"HOW ARE YOU FEELING?" I ASKED SOFTLY.

"Irritated," she replied, her blue eyes flaring.

I cocked a brow. "Irritated?"

"Yes." She stared me down. "I'm naked, Xai."

"I see that, Evangeline."

"Do something about it."

My lips twitched in amusement. "I would offer you my shirt, but I'm not wearing one." That seemed to be my constant state these days—bare feet, jeans, and shirtless. Oddly, I didn't miss my suits.

Her gaze narrowed. "You know that's not what I want."

I cocked my head to the side playfully. "What do you want, love?"

"Right now? To kill you."

"An entertaining proposition," I mused. "Try and maybe I'll reward you." It would serve as a dose of foreplay shrouded in a test of her strength. I refused to push her until I knew she could take it.

We didn't make love. We fucked. Hard.

I widened my stance and taunted her with a doubtful look.

Her resulting growl went straight to my groin. Coupled with her lack of clothes, well, my pants were suddenly feeling a bit tight.

"Having second thoughts, darling?" I took a step toward her. "Worried you might be out of practice?"

Dark Provenance Series

Son

OF

Chaos

USA Today Bestselling Author

Lexi C. Foss

Son of Chaos

Copyright © 2018 Lexi C. Foss

Line/Copy Editing by: Outthink Editing, LLC

Cover Design by Covers by Juan

Proofreading by: Allison Literary Services

Print Edition

ISBN: 978-1-7325356-5-7

To my grandmother "Jo" for believing in me and telling me to follow my dreams. You're forever in my heart and my very own guardian angel <3

SON
OF
CHAOS

DARK PROVENANCE SERIES
BOOK FOUR

Son of Chaos

A simple mission turns deadly as the Daughter of Death is kidnapped by an old enemy seeking revenge. Now it's up to me to find her and I will kill anyone who steps in my path.

The Son of Chaos isn't playing. I'm armed, I'm pissed, and I want my Evangeline back. It's time for Heaven and Hell to meet the real Archangel inside of me.

Everyone will pay.
Many will die.
Silver will slay.

And a new power will ascend from the Shadows...

A Note from Xai

I'm not nearly as good at this as Evangeline.

Apparently, you need to know about time and how it fluctuates between the realms. It's simple math—a day on Earth is a year in Hell. Similarly, a day in Heaven is a year on Earth.

Can we proceed now? Because I have a date with Evangeline and she's promised to let me play with her knives. Right, that might be stretching the truth a bit, but I'm going to play with her knives anyway and enjoy watching her try to stop me.

Until next time, darlings.

-X

XAI'S GLOSSARY

Angel: Superior beings, clearly.

Archangel: Angels at the top of the angelic hierarchy.

Dark Angel: Evangeline's adorable pet name for me.

Dark Provenance: A faction of Nephilim who want to protect humanity and need a hell of a lot of guidance from their superiors (Angels, in case you're not reading in order). Evangeline cares about them. So I do too.

Demon: Spawns of the underworld.

Divinity: Children of Heaven and Hell who work together to uphold the balance.

Fallen Angel: Angels or Archangels wandering Earth or Hell.

Halfling: Created when demons fornicate on Earth with mortals. Not common because they're frequently killed by Hell's minions for sport.

Nephilim: Created when angels fornicate on Earth with

mortals. Apparently, I'm in charge of an army of them. See above definition of Dark Provenance for details.

XAI'S DEMON DICTIONARY

Archdemon: Princes of Hell, otherwise known as demons who sit at the top of the demonic hierarchy. Similar to Archangels, but not as good-looking.

Cyclops: Giant demons with one eye and no brain.

Dargarian: Excellent bodyguards who breathe fire.

Demonic Lord: Reasonable allies on Earth who each maintain their own territory and all the demonic minions who reside within it.

Ghoul: Garbage demons who help clean up dead bodies by eating them.

Guardian: Commonly used as bodyguards for their brute strength, but their lack of intelligence renders them useless. See above definition of Dargarians for a security upgrade.

Incubus: Male demons who require sexual energy to stay alive and who commonly fuck mortals.

Ōrdinātum: A title assigned to demons who oversee specific regions within a Demonic Lord's territory.

Orsini Devil: Annoying little demons with a penchant for invisibility. Only to be used for spying when no other resources are available.

Pestilence: Archdemon Alastor's humanoid-looking pets who are known for causing plagues and other diseases. Not allowed on Earth for obvious reasons.

Portal Dweller: Extremely useful demons who can teleport easily between the planes but have a tendency to talk too much. Or at least Remy does.

Royal Guard: Cloaked demons assigned to protect the Princes of Hell, not that they actually require protection. It's more of a pompous status symbol. There is no equivalent in Heaven, and for good reason.

Scrubber: Helpful demons who erase memories.

Shadow: Wisps of former demonic entities that feed on life in the Shadow realms.

Slither: Evangeline's least favorite kind of demon because of their snakelike bodies and their penchant for ejaculating venom. Should be killed to make her happy.

Succubus: Female demons who require sexual energy to stay alive and who commonly fuck mortals.

Tracker: Valuable demons who can sense and trace auras. Always good to have one as a friend, unless they piss you off, in which case, kill the Tracker and hire help as needed in the future.

SON
OF
CHAOS

CHAPTER 1
HELL NEEDS NEW MINIONS

"Sloppy."

I whipped a blade toward the jibe and cursed when the bastard caught it by the sharp end. The dark angel tossed it aside with a flick of his wrist.

"Now that was just disrespectful," I accused. Silver didn't exist on Earth, making the item priceless. It deserved to be set aside with care, not treated like garbage.

My opponent shrugged. "Then perhaps you should consider improving your aim."

I narrowed my eyes. "If you wanted me to draw blood, you just had to ask."

Xai didn't smile. "Stop flirting and challenge me, Evangeline."

Arrogant prick.

I palmed two more knives and circled the tall, athletic, and sexy-as-sin angel before me. His all-black suit served as a taunt—a way of saying he didn't think I could ruin his expensive wardrobe.

Pity I had to prove him wrong.

He countered my leg sweep with a jump—just as I

anticipated. I swiped my dagger upward at the perfect angle to catch his thigh and grinned as it sliced through the fabric of his tailored pants.

I leapt backward, triumphant, and grunted as his palm slammed into the center of my chest. The concrete bit into my back as I landed unceremoniously on my ass.

"Shit," I breathed as stars danced through my vision.

"If you're going to ruin my pants, you might as well go for the femoral artery," he chastised. "I thought the Nephilim were improving your sparring, love, not worsening it."

"Fuck you," I managed as he straddled my hips and settled on top of me.

"Oh, we'll get to that," he promised, his ebony eyes grinning seductively.

He plucked the knives from my hands and set them aside before sliding his palms under my shirt to find the other two weapons strapped to my ribs. The last time we did this, he had left me armed and I destroyed one of his favorite shirts. It seemed he didn't want a repeat performance.

"You don't play fair," I said as the spots in my vision started to clear.

"What would be the fun in that?" he asked as he drew one of my blades down the center of my chest. "And you told me not to go easy on you."

I snorted. "Jackass."

"Now who is being disrespectful?" he asked, grinning. "You had a perfect opportunity to bleed me and chose to ruin my pants instead. I went for the kill, as any being in my position would when facing the Daughter of Death."

"Sweet talker," I murmured, amused. Because he was right. I could best almost anyone in a fight, thanks to my lethal heritage and affinity for sharp toys, but Xai almost always topped me. There were moments in our long history that I managed to beat him, but they were rare. And I wouldn't have it any other way.

Xai pressed the knife to my throat before leaning down to brush his lips over mine. "I think the Nephilim may need a harsher instructor, love."

"You'll kill half of them."

"They would recover. In theory, anyway." He didn't sound all that concerned. Then again, humanity never did matter much to him. A consequence of spending over two thousand years on this plane.

"Mietek said we're here to help guide them, not slaughter them," I reminded.

He sat up again, the blade still at my throat. "They are destined—" Xai's midnight gaze drifted to the woods surrounding our home as a prickle of energy tinged the night air.

Demon.

No, not just any demon.

An Archdemon.

Xai stood, alert. I joined him, placing my back to his, silver blades slipping into my palms. We chose this retreat for its elevation and exclusivity, giving us the ultimate advantage should any unwanted parties choose to disturb our dominion.

A swish of robes sounded to my left as several members of the Royal Guard appeared. The emblem embedded in their dark blue cloaks belonged to Ashmedai. He appeared behind them, his white-blond hair glowing in the moonlight, his sculpted abdomen bare, and a pair of board shorts slung low on his hips.

Xai was gorgeous in his own right, while Ashmedai

defied reason. Mortals didn't stand a chance in his presence. Hell, even I wanted to weep at the sight of him. And the way the stars seemed to shine down upon him as he strode forward didn't help matters.

"It's fucking cold up here," he said, his brows drawn downward. "I much preferred Miami."

"You're welcome to go there instead," I replied, smiling. "We won't mind."

Xai snorted, folding his arms. "Why are you here, Ashmedai?"

"You're so much like your father," the Archdemon murmured. "Always wanting to discuss business over pleasure." He drew out the last word with a twirl of his tongue and stared right at me, his intention clear. Xai didn't take the bait, his confidence just as high as Ashmedai's where seductive energy and looks were concerned. Their collective arrogance was almost suffocating.

Almost.

"Get to the point before others decide to join us," I said, twirling the silver blade through my fingers. "You know you're not allowed on this plane."

He shrugged, his hands tucked into the pockets of his board shorts. Most Archdemons wore their ceremonial robes, but not Ashmedai. No, he resembled a surfer, ready to hit the waves. "It's far easier for me to ascend than it is for them to descend."

Ashmedai stopped before us, power seeping from his aura in waves. The Royal Guard at his back was only for show. Archdemons didn't require assistance when they wanted to destroy something, and they didn't typically show up with an armed Guard either. Which meant Ashmedai needed something.

"Kalida has escaped," he murmured, as if reading my

mind. Hell, he probably could, which was why voicing my shock at his three words wasn't needed.

"How?" Xai demanded.

"A mystery I'm still trying to solve." Ashmedai's shoulders lifted and fell. "I'm more concerned about retrieving her at the moment, since she escaped to this plane. You're both going to help me find her."

Such confidence.

And so not happening.

I tracked her down after she framed me for a murder I didn't commit—her own—and that experience was enough to last me for an eternity. If the demons let her escape, then that was on them to fix, not me.

I gave Ashmedai the politest grin I could muster. "We're booked this weekend, but thanks anyway."

Ashmedai matched my smile with a dazzling one of his own. "I like you, Evangeline. Always questioning authority and thinking you have a choice."

"And I like you too, Ash. Always commanding and thinking I'll jump to obey. So adorable."

His Royal Guard bristled at the nickname and my tone, clearly not approving. Ashmedai's amusement merely grew. "Kalida escaped twenty-seven Earth hours ago, and I've narrowed down her location to this region. That should give you a reasonable start, but I suggest you stop delaying with me and start searching."

"You seemed to have misunderstood me. When I said we were booked, that was me rejecting your request."

"Order," he corrected.

"Request," I repeated. "Look, I caught her the first time, and you lost her. That fuckup is on you to resolve, not us."

He arched one of those arrogant brows. "Not even if I offer to let you kill her?"

I snorted. "As if I would soil a blade with her blood." I had the chance to kill her two decades ago and passed up the opportunity then. Why would I change my mind now?

"What about your precious humans?" Ashmedai drawled. "Think of the havoc she may wreak upon them as a starved Succubus..."

"Guilt trips, Ash? I'm disappointed."

His lips twitched. "You need more incentive, then?"

"Incentive would imply interest, of which I have none. Get one of your demon lackeys to track her down." I had better things to do—like train a Nephilim army to maintain balance on Earth.

"He has no one else," Xai murmured, his ebony irises flaring with ancient knowledge. "Her aura has disappeared again, hasn't it?"

Ashmedai merely stared at him, his non-reply saying more than words could.

Xai smirked. "Without an aura, there are very few competent enough to track Kalida down, and you need to solve your traitor issue in Hell before you can fully engage in hunting her down. That's why you're here."

Ashmedai merely shrugged in response, neither confirming nor denying the accusation.

"Still not seeing how this is my problem," I pointed out. Hell needed to learn to control their own and not rely on the Fallen Angels of the world. I was retired for a reason.

Ashmedai's lips curled, a sinister gleam entering his violet eyes, one that sent a chill down my spine. "I thought you might feel that way, Evangeline." Those words didn't alleviate my concern, and neither did the snap of his fingers that followed. "So I brought some motivation, you know, to make this your problem, as you so eloquently put it."

A Portal Dweller appeared with her arms wrapped

around a woman with rich brown curls and dressed in jeans and a sweater. Her hazel eyes were narrowed into slits at Ashmedai, her curses slurred from the gag lodged between her full lips.

Trudy...

Oh, fuck that.

My knuckles tightened around my blades. "I suggest you let her go, Ash, before I make you let her go." Archdemon he might be, but that Nephilim belonged to me. I took a step forward and found my feet cemented to the ground. *Fucking telekinesis.* Were there any powers this Archdemon lacked?

Ashmedai chuckled. "Now, now, I promise to treat her well. I merely meant to provide a reason for you to work with me, which I believe has been achieved now, yes?" He glanced at the struggling female, amusement evident in his features. "When my advisors told me of your protective feelings for this one, I had my doubts. Why would you care about a Nephilim? Perhaps I'll learn the answers from her captivity in my realm."

"She's a child, Ashmedai." Xai sounded and appeared far calmer than the situation warranted. I knew better than to believe the facade. Xai was at his most lethal when he feigned disinterest.

"A child?" The Archdemon studied the fuming female with far too much interest. "With those curves? Hmm, I think not." His violet gaze slowly returned to mine. "Evangeline, you track Kalida and bring her to me—preferably alive, but it's not required—and in exchange, I'll return your protégé. Fair?"

"Fair?" I repeated, my ire creeping into my tone. "You seriously have a death wish." Trudy was not only my protégé but also my father's favorite student. "Azrael will

7

have your head for this."

Ashmedai smirked. "Only if he can find me in Hell, sweetheart. Happy hunting."

He disappeared in a flash, his entire Guard and Trudy disappearing with him.

I gaped after them, my legs slowly remembering how to function. "Fuck."

Xai chuckled, his palm sliding to my lower back. "An invitation I would love to entertain, darling, but it seems we have a demon to find."

"I may kill her," I growled, referring to Kalida. "Just for the inconvenience." And I'd probably stab Ashmedai too for good measure. With a silver blade.

"A show I'll certainly enjoy."

"I mean it." I turned to face him. "And that Archdemon better not hurt Trudy."

"He has no reason to harm her, love. He needs her for leverage."

"Still, she's a Nephilim, Xai." Hell wasn't kind to heavenly beings.

He palmed my cheek, his gaze intense. "Trust in her to handle herself, Evangeline. She's trained under the best."

My father.

Me.

Xai.

She couldn't be better prepared. "How did Ashmedai even know about her?"

"How do demons know anything?" he countered. "She'll be all right, darling. We'll focus on finding Kalida—then torture and kill her—and have Trudy back in no time." He wrapped his arm around my waist, pulling me closer. "Now, shall we visit the armory?"

I sighed, resting my head against his shoulder. "You always say the sweetest things to me."

He kissed my forehead. "Oh, and Gleason mentioned something about new toys as well."

"And now you're just trying to seduce me," I accused, unable to stop the smile from lightening my voice.

Xai's dark energy wrapped around me, caressing my skin and heating my blood. "Always."

I tilted my head to gaze into his midnight eyes. "Want to hunt a rogue demon with me?"

"You know I do."

"It'll probably be bloody."

"All the better, love."

I smiled. I knew I loved him. "Then let's play."

Because Kalida was just given a death sentence.

Courtesy of me.

CHAPTER 2
WILL YOU SLAY DEMONS WITH ME? YES!

The silver blade balanced in my palm, its weight perfect. "I think I'm in love with Gleason," I admitted, my gaze on the etching of my initials.

"That's a shame since I'll have to kill him now." Xai handed me a pair of silver-infused heels and eyed my legs. "These will go nicely with a dress."

I snorted. "You would suggest that."

"Well, I was going to recommend modeling them naked, but we have company." His attention flickered to the doorway as our demonic allies arrived. One was smiling. The other was not.

"Why am I here if she has no aura again?" the grumpy Tracker demon, Tax, demanded.

"Because we may need you to track some of her former associates," Xai replied as he trailed a necklace up my arm. "This would pair well with the heels."

"Naked?" I asked, lifting my blonde hair.

"Yes." He deftly adhered the clasp before turning back to his friends. "We already started a list. Review it and tell me where they are." He gestured with his chin to the paper on the table.

Tax just stared at him. "Do I look like a dog to you?"

I cocked my head to the side. "You do have a hound dog's nose."

Xai smirked and handed me another jewelry box. "This is from me." His gaze went back to Tax. "Why haven't you started yet?"

"I hate both of you," the Tracker muttered as he picked up the list.

Remy cocked his hip against the table, his green eyes taking in all the lethal toys. "This is making my skin itch."

Silver was a demon's kryptonite, hence it being my weapon of choice and why the underworld eradicated the substance from Earth several millennia ago. Thank the Heavens—literally—for Gleason, my metal-obsessed chemist. The Nephilim had created a line of silver items just for me, in addition to bullets for members of the Dark Provenance, and a few special orders for Xai.

I palmed the box he'd just given me and opened it on a gasp. A gorgeous sapphire surrounded by diamonds rested in the center of a dazzling yellow gold ring. Not my usual metal color, but I suspected that was the point.

"The stone matches your eyes when you're in a killing mood," he said, removing the item. "And if you shift it just like this, a tiny syringe appears with enough silver for one potent strike. Gleason is working on refills." He slipped it onto my ring finger and brought my hand up to his lips. "Beautiful."

"Xai..."

Remy cleared his throat and pushed away from the table while muttering, "I almost miss the sadistic version."

"Welcome to the club," Tax grumbled, shuffling through papers.

I ignored them and lifted onto my toes to thank my dark angel appropriately. "You know me so well," I whispered against his mouth.

"It's about time you realized that." He palmed my ass, forcing me against him. "Kiss me."

"So demanding."

"Now, Evangeline."

I smiled and softly brushed my lips over his. He drew his hand up my back to my hair, his fingers knotting in my strands.

"Tease," he growled, his mouth capturing mine in a kiss meant to punish. My favorite kind. Harsh, hot, and so very Xai. Mmm. I tasted him back, my tongue dancing eagerly with his as he dominated me in every way. Only one man could handle me in this manner—all the others would die —but this being earned my submission.

Still, I couldn't help pressing a blade to his lower abdomen in reprimand.

"We have to work," I reminded him, sliding the razor edge along his dress shirt hard enough to convey my message without destroying his expensive clothes.

He caught my wrist in his hand and spun me, placing my back to his front, and caged me in his arms. "Then you should stop flirting with me, Evangeline." The words were a breath against my ear, his erection firm against my ass.

Insatiable.

"You started it."

"And you finished it," he whispered darkly. "You know how much I adore your penchant for knives."

"If you two are done, I have a location of interest," Tax drawled, breaking the moment.

Xai didn't release me as he asked, "Where?"

The Tracker gave us a look. "Take a guess."

"Miami," we both replied in unison, referring to the city we tracked her to after she faked her death and disappeared two decades before.

"She couldn't be that dumb," I added. "Could she?"

"I didn't track her aura there, just the one of Geier's former Ōrdinātums—Sharon. It's possibly a coincidence, but worth checking."

Remy popped up and loosened his neck. "Beach?" he asked, waggling his dark brows. "Let's go. I'm all for women in bikinis."

"It's the last place we would expect her to go after last time," Xai said slowly.

I snorted. "Because it's too obvious." Miami had been Kalida's point of operations when she tried to start a celestial war. Returning there was suicide.

"But that also makes it an ideal location to hide." Xai rested his jaw on my shoulder, his arms still solid as steel around me. "No one would expect her to be that foolish."

"And it is Kalida we're talking about." The same demon who tried to frame me for her own murder by leaving a rusty old blade with my initials on it at the scene. Not the brightest of demons. "If anything, we can see what Sharon knows."

Xai nodded. "A reasonable starting place. We can look for any of Kalida's old contacts while we're there."

"Except a lot of them are dead since it was over two decades ago," Tax put in. "But sure."

Right. Time warp. The whole one-Heaven-day-equals-an-Earth-year thing was really confusing sometimes. What Xai and I had enjoyed as a minor holiday trip back home had equated to over two decades here, changing everything and everyone around us.

On a similar note... "It's the last place Kalida knew before being sentenced to Ashmedai's realm for however many millennia has passed there." Since Hell worked in the opposite direction—where one day on Earth equated to a year in the underworld—it would feel like a heck of a lot longer timeline to her. "Maybe she did go back to Miami."

"It's worth investigating," Xai agreed, releasing me. "Grab whatever other weapons you need, love. I'll go make our hotel arrangements."

MY HEELS CLACKED over the marble as I did a slow circle in the hotel lobby.

The digital age certainly had done a number on customer service. No more reception desks, just booths where patrons could select what they needed. Xai hadn't needed to do much more than pay electronically before he was sent an electronic key that opened our door to the suite. After depositing our bags—something an automated service attempted to do for us—we wandered back downstairs in our evening attire.

"No forced interactions with humans?" he mused. "I approve."

I pinched my lips to the side, debating. "It's a bit sterile."

"And yet, far more pleasing." He held out his elbow. "Shall we, darling?"

"Chivalry?" I slid my arm through his. "Who are you and what have you done with my Xai?"

"He's waiting for you upstairs in the suite." He bent his

15

head, lips against my ear. "Might I suggest we finish this mission before he decides to engage in his penchant for exhibitionism? Because that dress would look far better hiked up around your hips, darling."

Delicious heat pooled in my belly as I glanced sideways to meet his smoldering gaze. "Is now a good time to tell you I'm not wearing anything other than two tiny silver blades beneath this very short dress?"

His resulting growl went straight to my lower abdomen, stoking the fire brewing there. "You're lucky we have somewhere to be right now."

"Or perhaps, *unlucky* is the better term," I replied coyly.

He nipped my ear hard enough to bleed and laved the wound with his tongue. "Careful, Evangeline."

"Never, Xai." What would be the fun in that?

His dark chuckle vibrated against my skin. "It's a good thing you're armed, love. You'll be needing those knives later."

"Promise?"

He nuzzled my neck. "Yes. Now let's get going before I fuck you in this lobby." He tugged me toward Tax, who stood waiting for us in an all-black suit that rivaled Xai's attire. My deep red dress would hide blood just as well and popped against my alabaster skin, making it a much better choice than the midnight dress code.

"Sharon is at a dance club about a mile from here." Tax turned with the words, leading us toward a sleek vehicle with two doors. They lifted before us, revealing the posh two-seat interior. He tossed the keys to Xai while spouting off an address and walked off, presumably to meet Remy somewhere for a ride.

"Why do you get to drive?"

Xai smirked as he opened the passenger door. "Get in the car, Evangeline."

I narrowed my gaze. "It's like you want me to stab you."

"Foreplay, love."

"Unless I render you useless with a well-positioned blade." I blew him a kiss and slipped into the leather interior, the fabric on my legs inching high to reveal as much skin as possible.

His lips twitched. "I dare—"

The crack of a bullet silenced his words.

I jumped out of the car just in time to catch him as he fell, a thin rivulet of blood streaming from the indent between his eyes. "Xai!"

He lay motionless in my arms as I collapsed to the concrete, screams lancing the air around us. I barely registered them, my attention on the unconscious male in my arms.

A too-fresh memory blossomed, one where I thought I'd lost him forever. His death an imprint still branded into my heart.

Not again.

I refused to lose him.

He's fine.

This couldn't be happening.

How? Why? Who?

A crushing reality, fracturing my soul in two...

Get it together, Evangeline.

It was too soon. I'd only just brought him back, only just agreed to finally be his. After so many millennia of working toward this—*us*—I refused to accept this fate. To even acknowledge the possibility.

Just a bullet.

Focus!

17

I closed my eyes, forcing my mind to override my heart. Swallowing my terror. Knowing he would be fine. He would wake up. It took a lot more than a gun to kill one of our kind. Even if it was silver, he'd be fine.

He's fine.

But the second I used to gather myself was too much.

A rookie mistake born of emotions and not the longevity and knowledge of my birthright.

I knew better.

Too late.

The barrel of a gun touched my temple.

A cruel laugh tickled my ears.

"Predictable," someone growled.

And the world went black.

CHAPTER 3
WELL, THIS SUCKS

Brimstone.

Sulfur.

Burning flesh.

All scents I recognized, but it was the delirious sensations that confirmed my location. My stomach heaved from the wrongness surrounding me, my mind fracturing beneath the weight of depravity.

Angels didn't belong here.

Not even the Fallen ones.

Xai, my soul whispered, longing for his strength through our ethereal bond. *Too far away*. I couldn't pull energy from him here—only the bare minimum to stay aware. Without my ties to him, I'd be lost in an unconscious stupor, suggesting I'd been in Hell far longer than ever before.

Had it taken me longer than normal to recover from the gun wound to my head? Because I was in Hell? Had I been shot or just struck?

So many questions.

Too little answers.

"I think she's waking up," a gruff voice announced.

Oh, you're a smart one, I thought back at him. *Well done, you.*

"Good," a harsher voice replied. Throaty and feminine, and not at all familiar.

Whom had I pissed off this time to warrant this little trip to Hell? The list was endless considering all the lives I'd taken throughout the millennia. A consequence of my job. For some reason, they blamed me for my having to kill their friends. If they had been good little demons who behaved, my job would have been moot. But no, they all had to go causing destruction on Earth and attracting my brand of punishment.

Damn demons. They never wanted to take credit for their own errors.

I would have sighed if my lungs were on board with the motion. The cloud of smoke didn't help, and neither did the stench of torture suffocating my nose.

Yeah, this was going to hurt. Especially considering I could hardly breathe, let alone fight.

I took stock of my bound hands and feet, the torrid air touching my exposed torso, and the metal chair beneath my bare ass.

Naked and in Hell. Not my proudest moment, but I'd survived worse.

A smack across my face had me biting back a curse.

"Oh yeah, she's awake."

Another smack had me glowering up at the hazy face above him. Words failed me since my vocal cords were coated by Hell's atmosphere, but I attempted to convey my irritation through my eyes.

"There she is," the gruff voice announced. He sounded like a dipshit, so I gifted him that nickname.

"About time," his counterpart muttered in that hoarse voice.

And I hereby dub you Shitmeister.

Brilliant. Now that they had names, they could die. Just as soon as I figured out how to move again.

A sharp tug forced my head back to stare into a messy blob. Pale skin, maybe dark hair. Couldn't tell. Seemed to be a big messy blob of humanoid demon. Blinking didn't help either.

"Oh, no, I want you fully engaged." Shitmeister followed the bitter words with another slap across my face. "Join us, Eve."

Sure. Just untie me and I'll happily hit you back.

Icy liquid shocked my bare skin as one of them dumped what had to be a gallon of water over my head.

Fuck!

Now, that was just uncalled for.

Another bucket swiftly followed, sending a jolt down my spine. And by the third one, my vision was clear and focused on Dead Man Number One, also known as Dipshit. His lips were stretched in a pleased grin, his hazel eyes brimming with pride at having doused the poor Fallen Angel in water.

Something about him struck a familiar chord. Was it the mane of dark curls? That lithe yet athletic build? The handsome lines of his face?

Hmm. I couldn't quite place it. Nor could I identify his demon heritage. *How odd.*

"She's awake now," he announced.

"And pissed," I added. "Good job." Because I would be killing him first after I freed myself.

The only positive of the water? I realized I wasn't nearly as bad off as I thought. Xai's essence pounded through my spirit, granting me the ability to function far better than most in my situation.

Which means he's definitely alive.

Not that I expected otherwise, except for that one moment of weakness. Fucking memories.

A chair scraping over rock pierced my ears. "Wow, that's a horrible sound." I winced as it increased until Shit-meister stood before me. A female, if the curves were anything to go by, and, yikes, she had a very unfortunate face with scars riddling every inch of her exposed skin.

She flipped the chair around and straddled it, crossing her leather-clad arms across the back, her gloved fingers tapping a rhythm. "Eve."

I met her dark irises, a note of recognition flaring inside of them. "Kalida?" I asked, shocked by her ghastly appearance. "You look like hell."

Her lips twitched, whether in a grimace or a grin, I couldn't tell. "That's what happens when you're tortured for long enough. You stop healing."

"Huh." I eyed her destroyed skin and the silver streaks marring her black hair. "It's a good look for you." And deserved after everything she'd done.

Another twist of her mouth. "I'm very glad you think so, Eve." She continued drumming her fingers, her head tilting slightly. "I remember everything."

I waited for her to continue, but she didn't. "Congratulations?" I remembered a lot too. Like her trafficking demons onto Earth as part of some fucked-up plan to dethrone her father and replace him with Geier, the former Demonic Lord of North America. That didn't go so well for her. Case in point, her face.

"Everything," she repeated. "The way they skinned me alive over and over again. Sometimes they burned my flesh.

Sometimes they let Ghouls feast on me just to watch me regenerate. Always awake. Always alive. Always remembering."

More of that incessant tapping. She clearly wasn't all there anymore. The way her eyes drifted upward, downward, to the side...

"They liked me aware, Eve. To feel. So many experiments. Eventually this became my permanent state." She gestured to her face. "It took a while, but as you know, time moves slowly in Hell." Another cock of her head, this one slightly eerier than before. Demented.

"How many Earth hours before Xai is healed, you think?" she asked softly. "Twenty-four? Forty-eight? It took you nearly a hundred Hell hours, which isn't even one Earth hour. Just think of the amount of time we'll have together while he recovers." She leaned in closer. "And then it'll take him far longer to ever find you. That leaves us plenty of years, hopefully decades, for me to demonstrate some of my most tormented memories. On you."

I stared at her, unfazed, waiting for more. If she thought I would weep or beg, then she'd caught the wrong woman. And the whole Xai-finding-me nonsense? As if I'd wait for him. I was the Daughter of Death, not a damsel in distress.

"Evangeline doesn't appear to be understanding me, Grant. Can you fetch me a blade?"

I glanced at the familiar male paired with the name. Still nothing. He left the room with a swagger in his step, his tailored pants and silk woven sweater denoting wealth.

Why do I know you, Grant?

And what kind of demon are you?

"I've dreamed of this for several millennia," Kalida mused. "Ripping you apart piece by piece, watching you mend, and doing it all over again. Scarring that flawless skin permanently, etching my initials into your face so Xai thinks of me every time he looks at you, burning your—"

"I'm just going to cut in and say that you probably need to seek some mental help, K. Seems like you're harboring a lot of pent-up anger toward the wrong person, when perhaps you should be looking in the mirror." I cringed mockingly. "Actually, on second thought, maybe not. You might break it."

Her fist connected with my jaw, shooting stars behind my eyes.

I laughed, genuinely amused. "You're right, K. We're going to need all the years you can get down here." Another meeting of her knuckles against the side of my head had me laughing harder. Not because I enjoyed being punched, but because it provoked her to hit me again and each jostle served as a chance to test my restraints.

By the time Grant returned, Kalida had hit me five times, causing my lip to bleed and my face to ache.

He watched as the warm liquid slid down my chin and dropped to my chest, his hazel eyes heating. "You look better in a bikini."

I stopped testing the bindings around my wrist and met his hazel eyes.

Bikini? Was that some kind of hint as to why I recognized him, or just an offhanded comment?

"Who are you?" No, that wasn't the right question. Who he was didn't matter. "*What* are you?" I clarified. Because he clearly wasn't human, but I sensed nothing demonic about him either.

His lips twitched. "Having a problem seeing my aura, babe?"

It dawned on me then, the missing piece of the puzzle we never actually solved about Kalida. I hadn't thought much of it after we caught her, had assumed the demons would figure it out, but no one had ever mentioned it again. "You're the reason Kalida's aura disappeared." I had no idea *how* that was possible, but the spark in his gaze confirmed it.

He performed an extravagant bow. "At your service."

"How?"

"Are you really that blind?" Kalida asked, her voice still holding that raspy quality to it.

The scarring extended to her insides, I realized. *Ouch.*

"I've been told your kind can't sense me, something that was proven when no one came after me a few decades back." Grant smiled. "One of the only gifts of my birthright."

"You're not a Halfling," I said, scrutinizing him. Because even a partial demon would have an aura. Only angels... *Oh.* My eyes widened. "A Nephilim?"

"Ding, ding, ding!" He actually clapped with excitement. Dipshit was clearly the better name for him. I wanted to roll my eyes, but I was too busy frowning.

A Nephilim. In Hell.

Impossible.

Xai was the only heavenly being I knew who could survive down here, and that was a result of him being the Son of Chaos. Our bonded souls—his essence—was what kept me aware here, but my inability to figure out these damn handcuffs proved how Hell weakened me.

It's just metal. I should be able to shatter it, but I could hardly move my arms, let alone yank them.

This is not looking good.

"Care to reward her, sweetheart?" Grant handed a sharp instrument to Kalida that more or less resembled a razor blade.

27

"Why?" I asked, ignoring the scarred Succubus and focusing on the child of Heaven.

"Why what, babe?"

My teeth ground together at the stupid nickname. He could at least be more inventive. I called him Dipshit, after all. Swallowing the urge to reprimand his lack of creativity, I asked, "Why are you down here?"

"Ah, that's a question for your precious Dark Provenance," he replied. "Which, sadly, I don't think you'll get to ask them. How disappointing for you."

The metal edge touched my thigh, scraping downward sharply as Kalida ripped my flesh without warning. And fuck, it hurt, but I didn't even give her the satisfaction of a grimace. As the Daughter of Death, pain was an old mistress, and she was going to have to do a hell of a lot better than that to garner a reaction from me.

"You've both lost your fucking minds," I said, my voice far calmer than the one cursing inside my head.

Another strip of my skin was added to the pile below, followed by a maniacal laugh from Kalida. "Prep the surgical room, Grant."

"Planning to give yourself a new face?" I asked sweetly while continuing to fidget with the metal encasing my wrists.

Why can't I find a weakness? Maybe when they move me—Fuck! She'd run the razor down my breast, snagging my... I couldn't think about it. Couldn't even look down.

Okay.

No, this wasn't working.

I needed a new plan.

Something to distract them, keep them talking, a way to break—

Fire licked down my abdomen as she started running

the razor repeatedly over my skin. My nails bit into my palms, my mouth forcefully closed, refusing to give in to the scream clogging my airway.

That would only grant her more satisfaction.

Kalida cackled, her face contorting terrifyingly into what probably used to be a smile. She started swiping at my skin at a rapid pace, slicing me open for her enjoyment.

"You're a sadistic bitch," I growled.

I hadn't deemed her worthy of my blade before.

I sure as fuck did now.

Electricity revved in the air as Grant reappeared with the tool Kalida requested—a bone saw. "Here, entertain yourself with this while I prep the other room."

She stood and kissed him soundly on the mouth, which he accepted far too greedily. As if they did this often.

That's not pretty.

And neither was the look she gave me as she returned with the very sharp surgical toy poised in her right hand.

Oh, shit.

"Now we can begin," she said, lowering the moving blade to hover above my sternum. "Try not to pass out on me, or we'll have to start over."

"Give me your worst, Kalida."

Her gruesome mouth twisted again. "I thought you'd never ask."

CHAPTER 4

I'LL FIND YOU, EVANGELINE

I grabbed a pillow and pulled it over my head, needing the ringing to stop. It was incessant and repetitive and fucking annoying. Evangeline must have hit me hard during our sparring session. I would have been proud if it weren't for the headache she left behind.

Paying her back would be fun, though.

"Xai." The voice wasn't the one I desired, so I ignored it. Remy would bugger off when he realized I didn't feel like chatting. I typically enjoyed the Portal Dweller, but he really needed to call first.

"Xai," he said again, this time with a shake of my shoulder.

Clearly, he didn't receive the subtle message. "Fuck off."

Where's Evangeline? I half expected her to hit him with a blade, just for interrupting us in the bedroom.

My brow furrowed at the thought, my hand removing the pillow so I could glance around the bed.

All white.

Cotton, not satin.

With a balcony overlooking the beach.

31

I sat up. "What the fuck?"

"He's up!" Remy yelled, causing me to flinch and throw a pillow at him.

"For fuck's sake, keep it down."

"Keep it down," he repeated. "Seriously? Someone shoots you in the head and takes off with Evangeline, and you want me to be quiet? Sure. Let me know when I can speak."

I blinked as Tax walked into the room with an electronic device and a coffee. He set the mug on the nightstand without looking at me, his focus on the screen.

"Someone shot me," I said slowly, trying to recall the last thing I remembered. Evangeline in a dress. The lobby of the hotel. Beyond that was a bit fuzzy. "Did you say someone took her?"

"Yeah." Tax seemed to be scrolling through information while he spoke. "And that ring your Nephilim made? The one I used to be able to sense an aura from? Nada."

I prodded the tender place between my eyes. "What?"

"Disappeared." He made a hand gesture while saying, "Poof. Gone."

Remy leaned against the wall across from the bed and folded his arms. "We've been trying to find her for the last three days while you recovered."

My eyebrows lifted. "Three days?" From a gunshot wound?

Tax finally lifted his gaze from the screen. "The bullet they put through your brain was one of those fragmenting kinds that poison your blood. Remy had to call Lord Zebulon for help."

"Yes, imagine my surprise to learn you all were searching for my dead-to-me daughter," a dark voice said from the doorway. The Demonic Lord of North America sauntered into the room wearing one of his trademark tailored suits. "Good to see you awake, Xai. Oh, and you're welcome."

Shit. Now I owed Zebulon a favor, which was never a good thing where Demonic Lords were concerned. Still, I managed a "Thank you" because it was warranted. "Tell me what happened."

"Someone shot you in the head," Remy supplied helpfully.

"This guy," Tax growled, turning the screen my way to show me a surveillance image of a man with dark hair.

I frowned. "I have no idea who that is."

"We didn't either." Tax hit another button, bringing up a document, and handed me the device to read. "But we do now. Or an alias, anyway."

I scanned the details, noting the records were over twenty years old. Grant McDowell, minor criminal in the Miami scene with no priors of arrest, just an extensive record of aiding others in the crime syndicate. More photos were attached to the file, along with a list of known accomplices and several familiar names. I swapped back to the surveillance footage and zoomed in on his face.

"Try the next image," Tax suggested.

I swiped over and growled. "He was at the pool that day with Streator." I didn't even recognize him, my focus at the time having been on Evangeline and our mark. "How is that possible? He hasn't aged a day."

Tax ran his fingers through his messy blond spikes. He really needed to consider a different hairstyle. "Yeah, we're working on that part. He's not human, nor is he a demon."

"That we know," Zebulon clarified. "It's possible he's from another territory or even the realms, but doubtful."

"Have you shown Ashmedai?" I rolled out of the bed,

ignoring my headache. We had a lot to do and little time to do it. "And do you have any lead on where this thing took Evangeline?"

"No to both," Remy replied. "After Grant shot you—from close range, by the way—Eve dove out of the car and sort of froze. He took advantage of the moment and shot her too. Then an unmarked car with tinted windows pulled up and he disappeared, with Eve."

I noted the point about an accomplice but focused on the more important statement. "Evangeline froze?" I paused in my pursuit of clothes from my suitcase and turned to look at Remy. "That's not like her."

"Nor is it like you to miss a threat right in front of your face," Tax muttered. "But here we are."

I cocked a brow at the Tracker demon. "Are you blaming me for this situation?"

Tax had the good grace to appear contrite. "I'm just pointing out that you both have been a little preoccupied."

"He means distracted," Zebulon said. "Which isn't the point, or relevant. Shall I contact Ashmedai's Royal Guard to request an audience?"

I almost scoffed at the notion but instead replied, "Yes." As if I cared about demonic formalities. The Archdemon showed up on my doorstep without notice. Why shouldn't I repay the favor?

I picked out a new shirt, jeans, and boots and went into the bathroom without a word to the peanut gallery.

Evangeline froze?

And how had I allowed someone to sneak up on me with a gun?

He means distracted.

I pondered that statement while rinsing the blood from

my hair and scalp and washing away the grime of spending three days in bed after being shot.

Were they right? Had my relationship with Evangeline put us both in jeopardy?

No, we're stronger together.

I knew that. She knew that. Three millennia of fighting our passion for each other had proven that we needed each other. I was only ever alive in her presence.

Where are you? I thought, reaching through our celestial connection, searching for my other half. A lingering hum of energy served as the only confirmation of her being alive.

I'll find you, I promised. *You're never alone.*

I shut off the water, dried off, and dressed.

Evangeline could take care of herself; that I knew. But Tax's inability to sense the aura we laced into her ring was troubling. The gift served two functions—a weapon and a beacon device for situations such as this.

"Is the ring destroyed?" I asked as I walked back into the main bedroom.

Tax had taken up residence on the bed, his legs stretched out and crossed at the ankles. He glanced up from the device in his hands and shook his head. "No. I would have felt that since we tied it to my aura."

"So she still has it?"

He considered, his lips pursing to the side. "It's possible someone removed it and put it somewhere, but that wouldn't explain why I can't track it. Like, I can't even sense the ring, almost as if it somehow died. But again, I didn't *feel* the destruction."

"Does it feel as if the life energy just disappeared without a trace?" Zebulon asked, his expression darkly curious.

"Yeah, like it just never existed," Tax agreed. "Weird, right?"

"No, that's what happened to Kalida." His chocolate gaze met mine. "Her aura came back after her capture, as if it had never left. We never determined the cause."

"Ashmedai had her in custody for how many thousands of Hell years and never asked?"

"He was more concerned with punishment."

Of course he was; all demons enjoyed a good bout of torture. Ashmedai probably thought it was irrelevant since she came back with her aura, or perhaps even forgot about it with all that ancient history clouding his thoughts. "Well, I'd say this is all related and Kalida was the one driving that car."

"Clearly," Zebulon replied, his voice bored. "She set it all up."

He said it with such finality that I had to raise a brow. "You have sufficient proof?"

"Aside from common sense?" he countered, matching my expression. I didn't respond, merely held his gaze and waited for him to elaborate. His lips twitched, the only indication that he enjoyed this old game between us. I requested more information, not a rhetorical response.

"Yes," Zebulon finally said. "Tax informed me you followed Sharon's aura here. I've already had a debriefing with her, and she claimed I summoned her to Miami for a meeting." He scoffed at that last part. "As if I would ever find her worthy."

"Someone used your protocols to contact her," I inferred. "And Kalida would be familiar with them."

"Right, she lured you into a trap and you all fell for it." Zebulon's voice held a disappointed edge that was more than deserved.

"We should have been more careful," I admitted, irritated. It had been too obvious—something Evangeline had even commented on—and I hadn't bothered considering the potential for it to be on purpose. I would not be making that mistake again.

Zebulon's focus shifted to his wrist as he hit a button on his watch. "Ashmedai has just agreed to see us."

I snorted. "How generous of him."

Remy pushed off the wall, while Tax remained on the bed. "I need to check something else," he said, that screen holding his fascination. "I have a program running to track Grant's images, trying to pinpoint his location, but he keeps disappearing. In this day and age of surveillance, that shouldn't be possible. I want to do some more digging while you talk to Ashmedai."

"You're avoiding the Archdemon," I translated.

"He scares the shit out of me." Tax flipped his screen to me again, displaying a convoluted map with pins. "But this is why you want me to stay here. I want to check these places for portal points, so I need to borrow Remy too."

"Taxi driver, at your service," the Portal Dweller deadpanned.

I ignored the banter and focused on the display of paths. "Are these all places where he disappeared from surveillance?" There were four consistent ones and a handful of outliers.

"Yep, and the nondescript car went here." He pointed to the purple dot. "We've already scouted the area, and it was just an old boarded-up gas station, but something disrupted the feeds. I want to find the common denominator to see if we can figure out where he took Eve."

"Careful, mate, or we might start to think you care about her," Remy said, grinning.

Tax ignored him, his light eyes on me. "I don't like not being able to sense her ring."

Because it made him feel like a failure. I understood. "Use your other means to locate her, and send me the files on McDowell. I want to show his face to Ashmedai to see if it sparks any recognition."

Tax pulled a phone from his pocket and handed it to me. "Already done, boss."

I smiled. "I knew you were useful."

"Yeah, you know, for digging bullets out of your skull, tracking down girlfriends, all sorts of things." His lips quirked up at the side. "Have fun in Hell."

"Always." I pocketed the phone and stepped toward Zebulon. "I assume you're going to portal us to Ashmedai?" It was a newer ability of his—only a few decades old—that had certainly come in handy. I could technically transport myself, but it hurt. Having him take us was far easier.

He held out a dark-skinned hand, palm up. "This list of favors is increasing, Xai."

"I'm sure you'll enjoy exacting payment, Zebulon." I grabbed his hand.

His sinister chuckle followed us into the dark spiral, the only indication that he already knew what he wanted from me.

And I wasn't going to like it.

CHAPTER 5
A DATE IN HELL WITHOUT EVANGELINE IS HELL INDEED

Chaotic energy flowed around us, invigorating my soul with every step as we made our way to Ashmedai's tower. The sapphire hues of his realm gave my olive skin an unnaturally blue glow, making me thankful for this being a temporary visit. I much preferred black.

"Why didn't you call me?" Zebulon asked as we ascended the stairs toward the front entrance. "She is my daughter."

"Feeling a parental responsibility?"

Irritation flashed in Zebulon's gaze, his lips flattened. Two could play the rhetorical game.

I opened the door with a grin. "Ashmedai came to us with the assignment, and we wrongly assumed it would take a few days to wrap up. Calling you wasn't really as high on our list as capturing Kalida so we could retrieve Trudy was."

"Tru," a female voice corrected from above. "I've told you that about a dozen times now."

"She's delightful, isn't she?" Ashmedai stroked a hand

down her hair as if petting a dog. Trudy caught his wrist and flipped it behind his back, pinning him to the balcony above—with his navy wings tucked between them.

"Shit." I vaulted the stairs as Ashmedai's Guard surrounded them, but a dismissive laugh from the Archdemon had his army pausing midstep.

"Pet me again, and I will kill you," Trudy growled, lifting his wrist to an angle that should have caused pain, especially with the way it flattened his feathers. I'd only ever seen the Archdemon in his true form once before. He usually hid his wings when he ascended to Earth.

"I might keep her," Ashmedai said, grinning rather than grimacing. "She's fantastic."

Trudy released him with a throaty grunt and took two steps back before crossing her slender arms over her leather vest. She glanced at the armed guards. "What? You want to try me next?"

"You seem to be thriving," I said, stopping by her side. Zebulon was still making his way upstairs, his expression bored.

"Thanks to a morning regimen of Archdemon blood." She narrowed her hazel eyes at Ashmedai. "Can I go now?"

"Do you see Kalida?" he returned with an innocent glance around. "Because I don't."

Those narrowed eyes turned to me. "It's been five years, Xai."

I counted the Earth days and sighed. "Indeed. Ashmedai, I'm doing as you requested. Perhaps—"

"I'll save you the speech. No." All signs of his playful energy disappeared behind the mask of a powerful being. "Now, why did you want a meeting?"

Zebulon finally reached the top and kneeled at the feet of his superior. "My Prince," he murmured, his head bowed in reverence. "Evangeline has been taken, presumably by Kalida and a male of unknown origins. We were wondering if you recognize him."

I retrieved the phone Tax had given me from my pocket and pulled up the image of Grant McDowell. Ashmedai took it, glanced at the screen, and shrugged. "Not familiar to me."

He started to hand it back, when Trudy snatched it from his grasp, her familiarity with the Archdemon evident. Ashmedai flashed her an amused look while everyone else held their breath waiting for a violent reaction.

Interesting.

"I know him," she said, frowning. "He used to be part of the Dark Provenance."

My eyebrows rose. "He's a Nephilim?"

"That could potentially be related to the aura issue," Zebulon replied, still kneeling. Until Ashmedai released him formally, he couldn't move. The Archdemon's keeping Zebulon there was a subtle way of saying he still held the Demonic Lord responsible for Kalida's bad behavior. Demons had a long history of grudges and punishment.

"Aura issue." Trudy shifted her focus from the phone to Ashmedai. "How would a Nephilim help a demon hide her aura?"

"Through a binding of souls," Ashmedai mused. "It would allow him to flourish in Hell and her to hide her aura. Fascinating that I didn't pick up on it before."

"But her aura returned when we captured her," I said slowly. "Are you saying she could turn it on and off?"

Ashmedai shrugged. "In theory. My blood has allowed Tru to flourish down here, as well as given her some other, unique talents." He winked at her as she scowled. "But I've not tasted her myself to see if her aura concealment can be borrowed or not."

"Try," she said, hands on her leather-clad hips. The whole getup was very warrior-like and rivaled Ashmedai's attire as well.

His lips twitched. "Careful, or I really will keep you, little angel."

I cleared my throat. "Your theory has merit, but the ring I gave Evangeline had an aura affixed to it that Tax can no longer sense."

"Then it seems your Nephilim may possess the power to shadow auras, which would make him related to Dariel, perhaps?"

The Archangel of Concealment. "I doubt he would appreciate that accusation." But I couldn't argue with the logic behind it. I'd have to ask him about his last visit to Earth and if he bedded any humans while wandering about.

"Right, I forgot. Your kind doesn't consort with humans." He stared pointedly at Trudy. "Nephilim exist by some other celestial magic."

"Right, so, Kalida is working with a Nephilim who may or may not have bonded to her and can conceal auras." Which meant we were no closer to finding Evangeline than an hour ago. I tried again to link to her, to find some way to locate her, but her soul only faintly whispered back. A confirmation that she lived and nothing more.

Come on, love. Fight for me.

I nearly pulled away when a whispering thought drifted through the bond. *I miss you.*

Everything froze, my entire focus on that wisp of her conscious. *Where are you?* I demanded.

In Hell. Clearly. And imagining your voice.

My heart skipped a beat at the dreamy quality of her

mental voice, so unlike my warrior, my better half. If I wasn't positive of our connection, I'd think it a trick, but I *felt* her soul brushing mine. My mate, my love, my life.

Where in Hell?

Too long of a silence passed before she whispered, *I wish I knew... I wish I could escape...*

Heavens, she sounded broken, as if she'd already given up. I palmed the back of my neck, my eyes still closed, my focus on the female I existed to adore. *Think, Evangeline. I need more.*

More what?

Detail, I growled mentally.

Confusion drifted through our mental channel. *Of what? Never mind. It doesn't matter.*

Evangeline, I snapped.

Nothing.

Fuck! The connection between us wavered, her soul leaving mine, wandering into the abyss of madness. What had Kalida done to her? If she was in Hell, that meant she'd been down here far longer than ever before. And if she hadn't escaped yet...

You've survived worse, I told her. But was it true? She'd never been in Hell longer than a few days, and who knew what Kalida was doing to her.

If Evangeline hadn't escaped yet...

No. I refused to follow that thought.

You'll survive this, I promised her, because there was no other alternative. I needed Evangeline alive.

I know... Her voice barely reached me, the connection closing without my permission.

My hands fisted at my sides as the urge to punch something overwhelmed me. Just a week ago, we'd been happy. Alone. Minding our own fucking business. And all that had changed because of a fucking Archdemon. My eyes opened to find the source of my rage standing before me.

He took a step back, but not fast enough to avoid my fist. His jaw snapped beneath the impact, sending a crack through the room and a jolt of shock to our peers.

Electricity fired through my veins as his Royal Guard reacted, their psychic energy pounding me at full force. I fed on their chaos, winding it around my being as my wings ripped through my back, unleashing my Archangel bloodline and dominating the room.

Fire singed the air.

Trudy screamed.

Demonic chants began.

I welcomed the fight. Encouraged it. Craved it.

The blue minions didn't stand a chance.

"Enough!" Ashmedai shouted, his command for his Royal Guard, not for me. "And, you, get up off the fucking floor."

Zebulon stood. "Thank you, My Prince."

"Evangeline is on this plane being tortured because you couldn't keep a measly Succubus hostage," I growled, stepping into the Archdemon's personal space. "I agreed to this mission because the task amused me and I had hoped to watch Evangeline kill Kalida. I am no longer amused, Ashmedai."

He flared his navy wings and settled them against his back. "Noted, Xai."

We stared each other down. His violet eyes to my black ones. Power sizzled between us. Fury. Authority. An ancient understanding.

"I was wrong before when I said you were similar to your father. You're far more powerful and intriguing than Mietek." Purple flames danced in his gaze as he weighed his options. It would be a fair match between us, even in his own realm.

But I had something he lacked: determination. I wanted his blood in payment for what was being done to my mate.

And he couldn't fight that.

"I'll help you find Evangeline," he finally conceded.

"You will," I agreed. "And when she drives a silver blade into your flesh, you will not retaliate." She wouldn't—*couldn't*— kill him, but she would stab him. It was the least he deserved.

He held my gaze for another beat, his lips twitching. "Accepted." He held out his palm, a line of blood already drawn. It served as a raw show of strength—Ashmedai was a powerful telekinetic.

That didn't intimidate me.

I held mine out to him and watched a similar path etch itself into my skin. We shook, blood to blood, vowing to uphold the deal.

The tension in the room fizzled and died, my wings gently folding against my back, but not disappearing.

A temporary truce.

Trudy stepped to Ashmedai's side, her hazel eyes wide as he draped a sapphire wing around her shoulders. "You've gone easy on us," she whispered.

I smirked—or tried to, anyway. She had no idea what I could do. Very few did. "Be sure to warn the others."

"Shall we get started trying to locate your mate?" Ashmedai asked, his voice bored. "Or do you want to punch me again?"

"Did it hurt?" I asked.

He blinked. "If I say yes, will that satisfy you?"

"Temporarily."

"Then, yes. It did."

"Good. I hope Evangeline drives a blade through your heart."

His lips curled. "Then I suggest we find her so that you can regain your amusement of our situation."

Not likely to happen anytime soon, not after the way she sounded in my mind. But her stabbing the bastard who put her in this situation would be a good start.

"Zebulon, can you summon Tax and Remy?" I worded it as a request out of respect, but I meant it as a demand. There was no point in the Tracker and the Portal Dweller searching on Earth with Evangeline trapped in Hell.

"Already done," he replied.

"Excellent." I held Ashmedai's gaze. "I hope you have an idea of where to start."

Darkness glimmered in his violet eyes. "As a matter of fact, I do. Through that unique connection you just used to talk to her."

So you do read minds. I always suspected it, but his comment proved it.

He merely shrugged. No comment necessary.

CHAPTER 6

WHAT YEAR IS IT? I'VE LOST TRACK OF TIME...

Voices floated around me, eliciting a pain deep within.

I didn't want to wake up.

Didn't want to endure another second of this madness.

Blood.

Bones.

Flesh.

I barely ate.

Barely drank.

Hell was not meant for my kind.

Or were we on Earth again? Kalida kept moving me, healing me, shifting me back, destroying me.

Xai... His name echoed in my heart.

My link to his soul was my primary survival. Without him tethering me to life, I would succumb to the darkness.

I thought I could outthink them, but nothing I tried worked. All my plans sank into an inky abyss, my mind fracturing beneath the torment.

When was the last time I fought? Or tried? How many years have I been here? Trapped in this plane of agony?

Come on, love. Fight for me. Xai's whispered voice almost brought tears to my eyes. So real, and so very delusional. I envisioned him beside me, holding my shattered soul and mending it with his love.

I miss you, I told him. Would I ever see him again?

Where are you? Three fierce words that I wished were real.

In Hell. Clearly. And imagining your voice.

Where in Hell?

I wish I knew... I wish I could escape... Was I even in Hell? The weight on my abdomen said yes. Sometimes it lifted. Those were the worst days. The ones where Kalida allowed me a glimpse of hope, a reminder of home, and ripped it away with a cruel laugh before sending me back to the underworld.

Think, Evangeline. I need more.

More what?

Detail.

I frowned. *Of what? Never mind. It doesn't matter.*

Everything I tried resulted in failure. Kalida had thought this through, had several millennia of plotting, as she so frequently boasted. I wanted to kill her. To shred her. To *destroy* her. But I couldn't even lift my hand. I was broken again.

The voices continued. In and out. Whispering. Yelling. Arguing. Laughing. At least three.

You've survived worse, Xai whispered, his voice growing faint. *You'll survive this.*

I know...

Or did I? I wasn't quite sure.

I yawned—or attempted to, anyway.

Shades of black painted the world, reminding me of a bed of feathers I longed to rest on again.

"I will break you, Eve."

My lips longed to twist into a smile at the frustration in Kalida's tone. Months, years—decades?—of this endless array of torment, and she'd yet to crack my spirit. My body, however, was a different story entirely.

Grant sighed. "She can't hear you, babe. You worked her too hard."

Not quite, Dipshit. I can hear you just fine.

"I know," Kalida growled back at him. "Take her back to Earth for a bit. I want her healed again. Faster. So I can break her again."

"Maybe we need a new method," he suggested. "Something more mental, as opposed to physical. Or a combination of both."

I pictured him massaging her shoulders while she spoke, both of them relaxing near my mutilated form. They frequently thought me dead and unaware, something I used to my advantage, constantly seeking a weakness. But while I had perfected this state of death, they always sensed my healing. Or perhaps timed it appropriately. The second my limbs tingled, they would start again, rendering me defenseless in an instant.

One of these times I would get it right. They would think me still incapacitated, and then I would pounce. I dreamed of that moment. Someday. Hopefully soon.

"What did you have in mind?" Kalida asked, sounding drowsy.

"Let's chat about it over dinner, hmm? Richard will guard her while we're gone."

Ugh, the Ghoul. I usually liked them. This one, not so much. Especially since he had a penchant for snacking—on

53

me. He was near the top of my kill list. Right under Kalida and Grant.

"All right," Kalida said, the sound of a chair scraping in her wake. "Just one thing first."

A sharpness pierced my chest.

Quick.

Harsh.

Agonizing.

I will kill you, bi—

~

VOICES AGAIN.

Louder now, two males talking about this week's agenda.

Grant and... maybe Derek?

Didn't matter.

My ribs ached, hardly healed, not ready for another round.

Don't move, I told myself. *Hide your healing. Let them think you're still dead.*

A male grunt. Something about agreement and a new torment involving my body in unspeakable ways.

No, my soul growled. *Only Xai.*

But I needed a few more hours.

Please. Not yet...

~

SILENCE.

What plane am I on?

I ached everywhere, but that meant little to me now. Pain was my mistress, my confidant, my being.

Charred flesh filled my nose. From myself? Because we were in Hell? I didn't know. Didn't care.

Did they say something about a new torture? Did it already happen? Nothing felt different, just my body mending itself. Kalida had done something to my ribs—I didn't care to think about what, but it hurt like a son of a bitch.

Yet, I could feel my toes. That meant another round would begin momentarily.

I waited.

And waited.

Are those my fingers? Fascinating.

More silence.

More sensation.

A clear breath slowly pulled into my lungs. Exited.

Nothing.

Was this the new torment? Allowing a glimmer of hope? Because I refused to accept it. After months—years—this was too far a deviation from routine. And I'd more than memorized the movement of my captors.

Well played, I thought at them. *But I see right through you.*

I refused to hope. It was a deceitful emotion. But if they wanted me to rest a little longer, I'd allow it. There were no restraints on my wrists or ankles. Maybe I could finally throw a punch. Even hitting Kalida once would be satisfying. Escaping would be better.

If they keep allowing you to heal...

No. I refused to consider it. That would allow hope to creep into my thoughts.

I remained perfectly still as the nature of my birthright slowly crept to the surface. That part of me clearly hadn't received the memo about not hoping, because now that I'd been left to heal beyond the norm, my assassin brain wanted to plot.

Fine. I could entertain the notion briefly, just to pass the time since I was still alone and unable to move.

I already cataloged the important factors about each of my opponents, their weaknesses and strengths, and general motives. However, the constant state of torture left me unable to act on any opportunities.

Not being tortured now.

True.

Hmm.

All that time under my father's tutelage, all my experience on Earth—there had to be something to use. My ring, obviously, since my captors never removed it. Likely because it was gold, not silver, and they couldn't sense the small silver syringe inside. It helped that Kalida liked the ring, said it reminded her of Xai and how devastated he would be when she finally returned me to him hideously scarred. Except, I kept healing. Oh, she hated the healing.

I would have smiled if my lips worked.

A shudder crept down my spine. I didn't want to stay here any longer. I wanted to fight. But that required moving.

Male whistling sounded from nearby.

Fake it. Don't let them know you're awake.

Because that's worked so well in the past.

Shh!

I slowed my breathing, a trick I'd nearly mastered in the last however many months or years. Maybe even decades.

Don't think about that now. Focus. That voice sounded mysteriously like my father's, no doubt a result of all the training indoctrinated into me as a child.

"I don't know, man, she still looks pretty dead to me."

The suave tone often spoke in my presence, but no one ever referred to the Portal Dweller by name. So I called him Sammy the Dead Man.

"Yeah, Kalida did a number on her, but the bitch should be more coherent soon. Then the fun will start." Grant's familiar voice had me fantasizing the ways I intended to kill him. Always slow, with a lot of blood.

One of them—likely Grant—ran a finger up my arm to my collarbone and down. "I have a Dargarian lined up for you first, Eve, darling. He paid good money. Something about you killing his brother."

If I did, he deserved it, I thought sweetly. *And lined up for what?*

"How do you want me to do this?" Sammy the Dead Man asked. "Portal her after each fuck to vary her location?"

Each fuck?

"Yeah, I'll message you the coordinates each hour. Just keep her moving and try not to let any of them actually kill her."

The Portal Dweller snorted. "I'm a transporter, not a bodyguard."

"Then I should probably play with her first," Grant replied.

It took all manner of thought and control to remain absolutely still as the finger circled my nipple, taking liberties with my mostly dead flesh.

Is that what you're into, Grant, you sick fuck?

Newfound desire to shred him cascaded through my spirit, livening my insides. My fingers almost twitched with the desire to find a blade, the most movement I'd felt in... forever.

I'm going to kill you all.

His touch moved lower, stirring bile in my belly.

I finally understood Kalida's desire, the plan Grant had laid out for her. Defiling my body on a sexual level to torment my mind and heart. Forcing me to embrace another that wasn't Xai. The worst kind of torture imaginable, especially for a mated angel.

Don't move, I told myself. *Don't react. You're not ready.*

But I wanted to scream. To break the hand touching me in a place it didn't belong. To shatter his fucking face with my fist.

You should have never let me heal, I thought darkly. *You should have kept me broken.*

Pure arrogance coupled with malice—they wanted me aware of it all, to be alive enough to remember. And that required healing.

This is my chance.

I felt it in every fiber of my being. Sammy the Dead Man planned to portal me around from conquest to conquest, confirming I was in Hell. That explained the nausea curdling my insides, the weakness I mistook for my body still healing.

I can feel my limbs, can curl my fingers into fists.

Not yet.

No, not yet.

My fractured thoughts should have concerned me; rather, they fueled my need for revenge.

"Not much point when the bitch isn't even awake," Sammy the Dead Man helpfully pointed out.

"You're right." Grant sighed, removing his hand—a hand I would be breaking today. "The Dargarian will be here soon. I'll go grab some adrenaline from the surgical suite to help move her along."

I almost growled. How many times had Kalida shot me

full of adrenaline before my body had finished healing just to rip me open again?

I'm going to shove that damn needle into your heart.

"Fucker," Sammy the Dead Man muttered. He did that often after Grant disappeared, which usually made me grin inside. Not today.

Move. Now.

My fingers curled, forming fists. It hurt. It was slow. But my hand *moved*.

I tensed my arms next. The atrophied muscle protested, shooting a spasm through my nerve endings. I did it again and again, needing to prepare myself. Subtle, small movements that the Portal Dweller would have noticed if he was paying attention.

My legs were next.

Running out of time.

I know.

Flex. Unflex. Flex.

It's now or never, Eve. He'll be back any minute.

I hated that voice, and adored her at the same time. My warrior soul finally coming to life and reminding me how to *fight*.

My limbs shook with tension, ready.

Time to breathe.

I inhaled as softly as possible, filling my lungs and exhaling, allowing my heart to increase in rhythm. Death thrived in my spirit. Now I called upon her to take over, to make me whole, to give me this chance at survival.

The Portal Dweller started whistling that creepy tune I heard in so many of my nightmares. He took me to Hell, to Earth, and back again. My soul reached for his aura, tasting all his bad deeds and malicious thoughts. It fueled my craving for justice in the manner of his death.

He will die.

Yes.

Now.

Yes.

I thumbed my ring, pushing aside the stone as Xai once demonstrated. So easy. So perfect.

It's time.

Yes.

My eyes slid open, the dim lighting welcome against my unused pupils. When was the last time I saw anything beyond my eyelids?

I blinked once. Twice. Definitely in Hell. No question.

My mark stood off to the side, still whistling, his focus on his phone. I debated warning him just to see the look in his eyes before I struck, but I didn't want to risk him teleporting before my reflexes took over. My fingers flexed, my arm poised.

Strike.

I put all my effort into that single movement, the ring angled outward, and grunted as it struck his forearm. I'd been aiming for his neck but couldn't quite make it.

"Shit!" He jumped back, but it was too late.

The syringe had punctured his skin, the silver streamlining into his bloodline. It might not be enough to kill him, but it would definitely render him useless.

His knees gave out as he clutched his arm to his chest. "Bitch!"

I tried to reply and couldn't. Rather than try, I forced myself to sit up, knowing time was running thin. Maybe three or four minutes had passed since Grant had left. He would be back any second.

Need to stand.

I swallowed—or tried—and swiveled my legs off the hard mattress.

Come on, Eve.

This was going to hurt. A lot. Fortunately, Kalida had trained my pain tolerance to accept high levels of agony.

Holding on to the bed as best I could, I slowly lowered my weight onto my feet and nearly fell from the difficulty. When was the last time I walked, or even stood? Didn't matter. I could now. I had to master it. Had to get the hell out of here.

My legs wobbled. I gritted my teeth, forcing myself to withstand it, willing my muscles to strengthen and accept my weight.

Sammy the Dead Man stilled on the floor, his face pale, but still very much alive. Dead demons turned to ash. At least he wasn't screaming.

I pushed away from the bed, testing my limbs, and found myself steady. A glance at the Portal Dweller showed no useful weapons.

Beyond him, a shiny array of knives caught my eye. Resting on the table was a set of freshly cleaned torture tools. Something for the Dargarian to use while he defiled my body, perhaps?

The thought had me taking a sturdy step, followed by another, until I stood right beside the array of pretty toys. I rolled my shoulders, feeling stronger by the minute, and plucked a blade from the tray.

Death rose to the surface, stretched her wings, and smiled.

Let's play.

CHAPTER 7

WOULD YOU LIKE TO DANCE WITH DEATH?

G rant was certainly taking his sweet-ass time. A quick survey of the room confirmed there weren't any surveillance cameras in here, meaning he couldn't know I had awoken.

What are you up to, Nephilim?

I twirled the blade between my fingers, pleased with the return of my dexterity. My muscles were twitching and protesting, my body sluggish, but adrenaline pumped wildly through my veins.

Death called to me. She wanted to play.

I tilted my head to the side, evaluating the ways I could assassinate Grant. It'd been a while since I killed someone. I welcomed him as my first victim.

Another whirl of the knife, this time faster.

The sound of footsteps had me pausing, my lips curling.

"Sorry, Kalida wanted a full report. She's at our next location playing with the bidders and—"

The knife flew from my fingers, nailing Grant solidly in the heart and cutting off his words before he even finished entering the room.

"Bull's-eye," I hissed, my throat dry and unused.

The syringe slipped from his hand and landed with a satisfying clank against the concrete floor. Grant fell to his knees beside it, his eyes wide with shock at seeing me standing before him. As a Nephilim, he wouldn't die from the wound alone. No, he required a far more brutal execution. But did I have time?

He teetered over with a soft thud, his mouth forming unintelligible words. A beautiful scene, truly. And so much less gruesome than he deserved.

In hindsight, I should have incapacitated him in a way that allowed him to speak because now I had no way of knowing how to get out of this literal hellhole. And of course, the Portal Dweller was useless to me as well.

Good job, Eve.

Better than being on that table.

Touché.

Well, there was no going back now. I picked up another knife and threw it unerringly into Grant's skull right between his eyes—retribution for what was done to Xai—and smiled as the dipshit lay unconscious on the floor.

I selected the three remaining scalpels and a shorter-looking instrument with sharp edges on either side and poked my head into the brown hallway.

Vacant. Not surprising. Kalida and her minions had done a great job keeping me hidden from everyone outside their fucked-up operations. But if the Dargarian was meeting them here, then he had either an entrance point or a Portal Dweller escort. Either way, I would be using that means of escape.

My legs cramped with every step, my stomach rioting at the wrongness of this plane. But I had to get the fuck out of here, to find a way to another part of Hell, to a realm with someone I knew.

Xai.

Ashmedai.

Zebulon.

Tax.

Remy.

I would even stand for Bael at the moment. Anyone.

A door appeared at the end, but I knew better than to trust it. Hell loved its tricks. No, I needed a nondescript exit, something plain.

All the low-hanging lights rivaled one another, not a flicker or a hint of anything out of alignment. The muddy walls—actual mud—were smooth and even. Dead grass lined the floor.

Where are you?

A few more steps, more studying of the lack of patterns on the walls and ceiling, nothing obvious.

Come on, come on, come on.

It had to be here somewhere. A misshapen blade of grass, perhaps, or… that weed. Clever. It was tucked into the ground, nearly hidden beneath the brown turf, but definitely there. I bent to brush my finger against it and gasped as I landed in a spiral of vines.

Greenery wrapped around my skin, hugging me, twisting and turning, and suffocating me amongst the leaves.

Shit.

This was why I hated the underworld. All these damn mazes and puzzles, nothing ever as straightforward as just stepping outside.

I sliced the scalpel against the rope of greenery, causing it to hiss and moan and release me into a patch of soil beneath a shroud of trees. Above it hung dual red suns, leaving me with no idea what realm I'd just fallen into.

My eyes closed for a second, my body aching from all the exertion.

Xai, I whispered, craving his chaotic energy. *It hurts.*

Where are you? Always the same demand. One would think my imagination might gift me a new phrase every now and then, but of course, those three words were very him.

Two red suns, I told him. *I'm so tired.*

Hang on for me.

I'm trying. God, those words hurt to think. He had no idea how much I was trying. Where was he? On Earth searching for me? In Hell? Did he know how much I was fighting to get back to him? Our relationship, while old, still felt remarkably young in so many ways.

I escaped, Xai. I willed him to hear those words, to know I'd finally done something right. He would be so proud. My lips almost curled at the thought.

You need to move.

I know.

No, I mean you need to move. Right now.

In a minute. I just needed one more second's rest. I yawned. They couldn't find me here. Not quickly. I didn't even know where here was.

Evangeline!

Love you...

Maybe I would dream of him. Oh, that sounded blissful. A proper sleep. Some distant part of me cried out in warning, shouting words about moving, running, leaving this plane... But I rather liked it here. The heat. The scent of Earth. Mmm. It really was quite pleasant. The best I'd felt in a while, really.

Dream with me.

Oh, I liked the sound of that.

Get up!

Why? This bed felt far more inviting.

What shall we dream about?

About Xai.

Don't you do it! Wake. Up!

Such chaos. Confusion. Alarm.

My eyelids lifted drowsily, taking in my darkening surroundings. What happened to the trees and the suns? They were shrouded in thick clouds.

I blinked awake, startled.

The fuck?

Everything around me was discolored in hues of blacks and browns, the air chilling to the coldest of nights.

Moss encased my limbs, gluing me to the ground—a sinister shadow lurking overhead.

My weapons were gone.

My body trapped.

My heart frozen in fear.

From one nightmare to another.

This couldn't be happening.

A tear tracked down my cheek, and something cruel laughed.

I hated this plane. This existence. This world.

"No," I whispered. "Not like this." Not after everything I'd just survived. To be trapped here, by this thing, in Hell's playground... It wasn't fair. But of course Fate would fuck me like this. She was such a damn bitch!

I pushed as hard as I could against the restraints, but they didn't budge. Didn't even crack.

That shadow loomed heavier now. Suffocating me inch by inch. So cold. So very, very cold.

Don't sleep. Xai's voice again. *Don't you fucking sleep.*

I didn't feel drowsy or exhausted so much as defeated. After everything... Oh, hell, I didn't even have the energy to consider it.

None of it mattered.

Not anymore.

I love you, Xai. I had no idea if he could hear me, but I hoped he could, hoped for once this connection was real. *I fucking love you.*

Don't you dare say your goodbyes, Evangeline. Hang on for me.

Tears gathered in my eyes, my lungs fighting for air. I couldn't move, could hardly breathe... *I'm trapped, Xai.*

I'm coming.

I wish that were true. But it was a nice thought anyway. My mind's way of soothing me one final time. *I'm so sorry, Xai. So sorry for all the time we wasted. I love you.*

Stop. If you give up on me, I will kill you myself.

I nearly laughed. How very Xai to threaten me now, in my final moments. *I picture you perfectly.*

I'm here.

A part of you will always be, yes.

Evangeline!

I love you, Xai... Always... Forever... Remember me.

CHAPTER 8

CHAOS LURKS WITHIN THE SHADOWS

F or the first time in my very long existence, my heart stuttered. I could feel Evangeline's energy slipping from our bond, her life disappearing right before me.

Evangeline!

No reply.

"There!" Tax shouted into the chaotic oblivion of Hell's realms.

Remy stopped, releasing us into the Shadow realm—a shady world where demons were sent to die. All the beings here thrived on the essence of the living, sucking their prey dry much in the way a Succubus would a human mate.

"I can't stay here," Remy said, his breathing already slowing. "Xai..."

"Take Tax. I've got this."

"But you can't—"

"Go!" I demanded, my wings extending and taking me into the smoggy air. I didn't need to worry about them when I had Evangeline to find. Her mental voice no longer replied to mine, her life hanging by a thread.

I was going to kill her when I found her.

And hug her for eternity while never letting her go.

Had Kalida left her here to die? After nearly a year of trying to reconnect to Evangeline's mind and find her, the aura of her ring had finally registered. Tax had relayed the location just as her soul had called to me.

I cut through the eerie clouds, calling to the chaos of this realm to expedite my flight as I scanned the ground for signs of Evangeline.

Where are you, love?

No reply.

Don't do this to me. Not after everything we've been through.

She had to survive. I required it.

Wisps of her soul grasped at mine, her essence struggling to keep her alive by any means necessary. I blasted everything I could through the bond, commanding her to live. I would not lose her. Not like this.

Negative energy spiked at my aura, the shadows trying to pull me down, but I sliced through them with ease, my Archangel bloodline giving me the energy I needed.

There!

A thickening smog descending on the trees.

I cut toward it, my wings simmering in protest from the abrupt turn. I pushed myself harder, sprinting toward the dark mass and splitting through the middle.

Shrieks littered the air, the Shadow demons displeased by my interruption, but my sole focus lay with the stray strands of blonde hair twined in the soil beneath them. A forceful beat of my wings had the creatures backing off, their chatters of annoyance mingling with fear.

"Leave." One word, underlined with all the power of my heritage. A being of Heaven I might be, but my birthright reigned over this dominion. One flare of my wings sent them all scattering, their terror feeding my energy shields and giving rise to the Archangel within me.

Electricity hummed beneath my fingertips as I waved them over Evangeline's form, mentally dismantling the vines and shrubbery that had captured her against the Earth. They unfolded under my command, revealing her frail, bloody form beneath, her body so much thinner than it should be.

I lifted her lifeless form into my arms.

"I have you, love," I murmured, my wings propelling us upward. "I have you."

She didn't move.

Didn't breathe.

Her heart didn't even beat.

My soul caressed hers, urging her to hold on, to trust me to fix this, to not give up on us yet. Evangeline needed more than this world could give her, more than Earth as well. She required the heavenly essence.

Fire encased our beings, singeing my feathers to ash as I teleported us between the planes. Ascension from Hell to Heaven required the most powerful of souls. Very few could accomplish it, most avoided it due to the energy cost, but we had no other alternative. Evangeline's light was nearly extinguished, her body too fragile to heal anywhere else.

Raphaela.

I telepathed the name on repeat as we ascended, knowing someone in Heaven would hear me and find the female we needed. Evangeline's mother—the Angel of Healing.

My back screamed in agony as my wings tore through my skin once again, replacing the ash with bold black feathers that thrived in their rebirth, my soul finally home.

But Evangeline remained limp in my arms, her body too weak to transform to her rightful form. My heart ached with the implication, terrified that I may never see those gorgeous violet plumes in flight again.

"Xai!" My father's voice came from afar as I landed roughly on Heaven's surface, the dense grass cushioning our fall.

I rolled to my back, cradling Evangeline tight against my chest.

Wind whooshed through the air as several angels landed around us, the leader one with dark brown wings with a span that rivaled my own. "What happened?" my father demanded.

"Shadow realm."

"How long?"

I shook my head. "I don't know. Hours, maybe days?" Time in Hell withheld reason, and who knew what Evangeline had endured before Kalida dropped her in the wastelands.

Another ruffling of feathers sounded as Raphaela landed beside my father, her gray eyes on her daughter. She gracefully sank to her knees, her hands going to Evangeline's face, her shoulders, her arms, and rearranging her so her back was against my chest, her head resting just below my chin. My hands fell to her hips, holding her against me, refusing to let go, refusing to lose her.

Come back to me, love, my heart whispered. *Please.*

Anguish discolored Raphaela's features, her lips trembling as she lowered her forehead to Evangeline's blood-coated chest.

"So much pain," she hissed. "So much to heal." The words were a rasp in the warm air, everyone silent as the only angel capable of healing Evangeline focused on her task.

Don't you dare let go, my soul growled. *You know I'll follow you, Evangeline. I've always followed you.*

A spark trickled through our connection—there and gone in a blink, but definitely there.

I closed my eyes and touched my head to hers. *Are you hearing me, Evangeline? You will not give up. You will fight. Or I will come after you and kill you again.*

Another tingle of awareness.

My hands fisted against her hips, my heart in my throat. *More, Evangeline. I need you to give me more.*

"Keep talking to her," Raphaela said softly. "I feel her responding to it."

You'll respond to your mother but not to me? I'm offended, love. I thought we were mates.

A mental sound that resembled a snort rolled through my mind, caressing my spirit.

You'll need to do better than that, darling. I realize you're out of practice, being retired and all, but my expectations for you have always been high. Now stop fucking about and come back to me before you really piss me off.

Annoyance filtered through the bond, whether real or not, I pursued it, taunting my angel in a way I knew would rouse a reaction.

Is that the best you can do, sweetheart? Because I'm disappointed, truly. What happened to my warrior mate? Have you lost your killing drive as well?

A low growl slipped into my thoughts. *You...* Her mental voice, so faint, so very real, had me clutching her sides, holding on for dear life.

What about me? My mental voice held a touch of a scoff

that didn't match the flutter taking off in my chest. *Do you have something to say? Finally?*

Kill... you...

And how do you intend to do that, love? By remaining weak and unconscious? Seems quite doubtful.

... ass...

I smiled. *You adore it.*

... missed you...

All amusement at her resurfacing died, replaced by the deep ache I'd spent nearly a year trying to hide. *I missed you too, Evangeline. So fucking much. Please come back to me.*

A pause had me holding my breath. *Keep begging. It's nice.*

I laughed out loud, my lips in her hair. *You cheeky minx.*

Mmm... adore it.

My lips twitched at her parroting my words back at me. *I do, love. Don't leave me.*

Never.

Because I'll follow you, I promised her. *You'll never escape me.*

I know.

Good. I kissed the crown of her head, relaxing. *I'm never letting you go again, Evangeline.*

Okay, she whispered, her soul mingling with mine. *I love you, too.*

I sighed, my cheek resting against her matted hair. While her voice was stronger now, her body remained frail and broken against mine, a sign of a long healing to come.

"She's going to be all right," Raphaela murmured, confirming what my heart knew. "Just keep lending your strength, Xai. Your bond is what's keeping her alive."

"No," I said softly, my arms wrapping around Evangeline's waist. "Her warrior soul is what's keeping her alive. I'm just her anchor."

~

I GENTLY BRUSHED the strands away from Evangeline's forehead. *I'm here.*

She hadn't responded or moved in three days, not even when I bathed and clothed her. Raphaela predicted it would take at least a week before Evangeline's spirit fully healed—the Shadows had clearly enjoyed feasting on her angelic light.

A whisper of air preceded my father's landing beside me on the balcony, his black-and-brown wings high on his back to avoid touching the marble patio. His penchant for elegance defied our chaotic heritage, which was likely why he did it.

I rose, my own feathers brushing the marble ground as I stood before him in a pair of black jeans and nothing else. Had I known we were expecting company, I might have dressed for the occasion. Then again, probably not. "Father."

"I just spoke to Azrael." No greeting. No inquiry about Evangeline's well-being. Just a formal statement and right to work. Typical Mietek. "No news on Kalida's or Grant's locations, confirming they are likely hiding in Hell somewhere. Of course, Ashmedai hasn't reported any updates on his progress."

"He hasn't determined who betrayed him yet?" How many years had passed in Hell since Kalida's escape? Over a thousand, maybe? I'd lost track of time going between Earth, Hell, and Heaven, and fuck if I wanted to do math now.

"If he's discovered the culprit, he hasn't deigned to comment. For all we know, he's already caught Kalida and just forgot to tell the rest of us."

"Doubtful." I drew my knuckles down Evangeline's warm cheek to her neck. "Ashmedai would wish to make an example of her, which requires an audience. We would know if he'd caught her."

"I agree." The low response floated on the wind as flames erupted in the air. Ashmedai stepped onto the balcony as though walking through a door, his wings only slightly singed from the teleport. Trudy followed him, her hair slightly windswept, her hazel eyes no longer holding the youth I once knew.

I was about to ask how long she'd been in Hell when my father snapped his wings out menacingly and took a step toward Ashmedai.

"Bringing a Nephilim into Heaven?" he growled. "Have you lost your mind?"

Ashmedai cocked his head to the side. "Don't like to have your dalliances on Earth flaunted about before you, Mietek?"

My father's dark gaze narrowed. "She's not mine." He spoke the words as if they tasted bitter.

"Oh, I'm aware," Ashmedai replied. "It's quite clear to me where her bloodline stems from." His lips twitched with a secret as he sighed, "Alas, that's not why we're here. I believe you were just discussing my inability to find Kalida?"

Of course he was listening. How, I had no idea. The Archdemon continued to defy the normal realm of power, confirming a suspicion I had several decades ago about the shift of energy in the underworld. Zebulon, too, had gained additional abilities.

"Yes, care to elaborate?" My father sounded bored, but the tension in his legs told me he was very much on guard. Archdemons didn't visit this plane unless they possessed a devious purpose, and Ashmedai proved himself more of a threat every time I saw him.

"She's not my primary concern at the moment," Ashmedai replied. "We'll find her, but there are far more pressing matters for us to discuss. Tru, would you care to elaborate since you demanded we make this trip?"

I startled, surprised that he would defer to a being so much younger than him. But as she eyed Evangeline's prone form, her expression devoid of emotion, I caught the air of *age* coming from her being.

"She's not recovered yet?" she asked, her voice holding a sultry note that spoke of confidence and experience. "I had hoped to talk to her too."

She sighed, her arms folding as she braced herself near the edge of what I knew to be a fifteen-story drop. Not a smart place for a being without wings, yet not an ounce of fear colored her features. No, she appeared hardened to it, as if she frequently found herself in difficult situations. Just as there hadn't been any sign of hesitation when she stepped through that portal behind Ashmedai.

That could only mean...

"You never allowed her to leave," I said, meeting the Archdemon's violet gaze. "Trudy's been in Hell this entire time?" *For how many hundreds of years?*

His lips twitched. "We have an arrangement."

"Tru," she corrected. "And it's not important. Will Eve be all right?"

"She'll survive," I replied, my attention still on the Archdemon. "You haven't figured out who betrayed you, and you haven't found Kalida. Why? Because you craved a reason to hold on to a Nephilim as one would a pet?"

"Did you just refer to me as a *pet*?" Now Trudy—excuse me, *Tru*—sounded irritated. What the fuck happened to the little girl who used to adore me?

"Careful," Ashmedai mused. "She can be scarier than me."

I shook my head. "Un-fucking-believable. Why didn't Azrael handle this?" The question was for my father, who had moved to stand near the edge of the railless balcony.

"Azrael tried," he replied. "Tru refused to leave."

"We're not here to talk about me," she cut in before I could comment on that. "I've discovered something we need to discuss."

I studied the woman I once saved from a human-trafficking ring and found a warrior staring right back at me. Evangeline would approve. Or kill Ashmedai. I wasn't quite sure.

"She's here as a favor," the Archdemon added. "I suggest you listen to her."

"All right." My father leaned against the wall, his wings tucked upward primly as he folded his arms over his chest. "Start talking, Nephilim."

CHAPTER 9

DEAR EVANGELINE, WAKE. UP. SINCERELY, XAI

I stood on the balcony long after Ashmedai and Trudy left, my gaze on the bright blues of the horizon.

"You miss it, don't you?" Raphaela asked from beside Evangeline. She'd stopped by to deliver her daily dose of healing energy, which was really more an excuse for her to spend time with her daughter.

A flurry of young angels took flight from a school nearby, causing my heart to ache. "I miss it every day," I admitted softly. "Evangeline does too."

"I know." Her mother stood to join me at the edge, her pale white wings a stark contrast to my ebony feathers. "But you're her real home, Xai. Evangeline would never be happy here without you."

"Just as I would never be happy here or anywhere without her." All those millennia spent pushing her away, trying to force her to live a better life *here*, had been at the detriment to my own soul. I never wanted her to leave me, but I never wanted her to Fall for me either.

Alas, Evangeline always did what she wanted.

Such as sleep for days on end.

I glanced over my shoulder and shook my head. "She needs to wake up."

"She's not ready yet."

"The Dark Provenance need us."

Raphaela smiled. "Azrael has them well prepared, Xai. Trust me."

"You've been to see him recently?" I had meant to check in, but I couldn't leave Evangeline. If she awoke without me by her side... No. I refused to allow that to happen.

I'm never leaving you again, love. Ever.

"Yes, just this morning, actually. They'll be all right. There's time." She patted my arm, an act few would dare do, but I welcomed the comfort. "You and Evangeline have given up so much for everyone else. No one would blame either of you for needing a break."

I sighed. "Now just isn't the right time." Especially with the information Trudy had just divulged.

"I'd say it's the perfect time," Raphaela countered. "You've handled everything for nearly three thousand Earth years. Let some of the others have some fun upholding the balance. Gives Ezra something to do."

I snorted. "Pretty sure he has his hands full." Or that was the rumor, anyway. I hadn't seen him in a few decades —not since that random meeting in Hell. Oh well, not important.

"Perhaps, but the Divinity exists for a reason, son. Trust in their purpose. "

Son. I merely smiled at the endearment. There was a time when this woman hated me. She'd never admit it out loud, but I sensed it from her all those years ago when she caught Evangeline and me together for the first time. Raphaela had not approved of her daughter's infatuation. Not one bit.

"Or better yet, why not let Fate take the reins for a bit?" she added, her light eyes twinkling.

I smiled at the reference to my mother—the Archangel of Destiny. She had stopped by last night with some of Evangeline's favorite baked goods, saying I'd need them soon. I translated her eerily Delphic statement to mean that my mate would definitely be waking earlier than anticipated. Sometimes it paid to have a mother who could predict the future. If only I'd inherited the same genetics.

However, there was one thing I knew for certain.

"We won't intervene until Evangeline is completely healed," I promised Raphaela. "But you know she'll insist on going to their aid." Evangeline harbored a soft spot for the Nephilim and all of humanity, something I admired about her, as I did not possess the same emotional inclination.

"Then it's your job to keep it from her until she's ready."

Amusement flirted with my thoughts. "Ah, Raphaela, if you only knew how impossible of a task that truly is."

"Oh, come now, Son of Fate and Chaos. We both know that's not true. What is it my daughter calls you? A 'cryptic ass'?"

I chuckled. "That is one of her favorite pet names for me, yes."

"Then channel that." She winked and patted me on the arm again. "I'll be back in the morning to check on you both. Until then, try to get some sleep. And maybe consider cutting your hair." She eyed my head with a mother's distaste before lifting in a flutter of white feathers. "That look is very last century, Xai."

I shook my head, smiling, as she disappeared from view. How a female could make me feel so young, I had no idea.

"Your mother still finds ways to chastise me after all

these years, Evangeline. And here I thought it was your father you inherited your strong will from." I ran my fingers through my long hair and shrugged. "I kind of like it. We'll see what you think when you wake up."

I kept hoping that each time I spoke, she would reply, but a glance at her peaceful form showed no signs of stirring.

I lay beside her and pulled her into my arms.

"This life is boring without you, Evangeline," I whispered, my lips at her ear. "Come back to me."

STARS FILLED THE NIGHT SKY, so different from those on Earth—more vibrant and lively. I admired them with a longing deep within my soul. Being away from home was always hard, yet being reminded of everything I'd given up was harder.

I relaxed on my back, feathers splayed around me in the plush grass.

Another day had come and gone without a word from Evangeline. I'd taken her out here, hoping it would somehow stir her from this incessant coma, but she remained just as still beside me, her blonde head using my wing as a pillow.

"I'm starting to think I've been too easy on you," I said softly. "What happened to my sarcastic assassin?" A part of me feared that Kalida had truly broken her. The other part knew Evangeline was indestructible. She could be hurt, yes, but never destroyed.

I sighed. "Oh, darling, the things I'm going to do to you when you finally wake up." When Tax had showed me the footage of her capture, I couldn't believe my eyes. She really did hesitate. "You clearly need more training," I growled, thinking back on it. "He walked right up to you, Evangeline." I shook my head. "What were you thinking?"

The night bathed us in silence. That's why we loved this field. Others rarely ventured this far away from the main cities, preferring the company of others. This was our private sanctuary, a place we often escaped to in our younger years to avoid detection. A relationship between us hadn't been forbidden so much as frowned upon.

My lips twitched with the memories of how we—

Energy hummed through the air, putting my senses on high alert.

Trudy's discovery about the shifting of power had put me on edge. Wars in Hell had a tendency to spill into the other realms, especially Earth, which disrupted the balance. Raphaela told me to trust the Divinity, but I knew better. There'd been unrest within that circle since Ezra ventured into Hell with that Halfling—the Heiress of Bael.

The hairs on my arms stood on end, forcing me to sit up and tuck Evangeline beneath my wing.

Something was coming.

Electricity sizzled through my veins, feeding on the pending doom.

Fire glinted across the sky, a warning from the Sentries —the angelic guard. Some things never changed, such as their late responses to intruders.

"Xai?" Barely a whisper.

I lifted my feathers to find Evangeline gazing up at me groggily.

"Of course you chose now of all times to wake up." I was almost amused, but the sense of dread had my lips refusing to curl.

Her rising now couldn't be a coincidence. It was her soul forcing her to move.

"What...?" She coughed, her throat working as her voice failed her.

Boom!

The crash had me rising to my feet, my eyes going to the flash of light cascading over the city. "Questions later, love." I held out a hand. "I don't suppose you can stand?" I meant it as a rhetorical question, knowing full well she was hardly awake, let alone physically ready to move.

"Xai." My name from her lips sounded painful, and when I caught the frustrated tears in her gaze, my heart gave an unsteady beat.

Weakness was her kryptonite. She hated relying on anyone other than herself, would prefer to live through the pain than to ever ask for help, and despised that she needed me now.

Another explosion rocked the foundation around us, but my focus was solely on her. I knelt, wings brushing the grass, and captured her face between my palms. "You are the strongest woman I've ever known and the most stubborn being of my existence." I brushed my lips against her forehead, my arms sliding beneath her shoulder blades and her knees. "You're my reason, Evangeline. You know that, right?"

She nodded against my shoulder as I lifted her from the ground, her breaths shudders of pain.

"I have you, darling." I kissed her hair, pausing to hold her tight. "You can hide with me. No one will know. I vow it."

Another nod followed by a sniffle that sent an arrow through my chest.

With a powerful thrust of my wings, I pulled us into the

night, my dark feathers blending our bodies into the sky. Gunfire and shouts rent the air, fire glistening in the distance.

A day in Heaven was over three centuries in Hell.

What the fuck had happened down there?

Was Earth caught in the middle?

I flew us toward the mountains, away from the turbulence behind us, and landed near a cave with views of the horizon. Evangeline remained still, but her alert gaze confirmed she was very much awake.

"Trudy and Ashmedai stopped by just yesterday with a warning that this might happen. There's been some shifting of power in Hell, something that's been coming for a while." That was why Ashmedai had stopped looking for Kalida; her disappearance paled in comparison to the disturbance on his plane. "The underworld realms have more or less moved."

"How?" she asked, her voice a hoarse whisper.

"We don't know, but we believe it's a result of Archdemons acquiring certain influential entities." Such as Ashmedai capturing Trudy. "They've disturbed the balance by bringing beings of Heaven into Hell." I set her on the ground and propped her up against the cavern wall.

The battle in the distance hardly reached our ears, but the sensations of it rolled over me, calling to my soul to intervene.

"Go." A slight command underlined that word, despite its raspy quality.

I smiled. "I can't leave you, darling."

She narrowed her gorgeous blue eyes. "Now."

A chuckle escaped me despite our circumstances. "Even half-alive, you're still trying to order me about. That's adorable considering it rarely works when you're at your best."

Evangeline was full-blown glowering now. "Xai."

The chastisement only amused me more. "Your mother told me to let them handle it, and I promised not to intervene until you were healed. I also told her you would never allow it. Seems I was right."

"Go," she repeated, and it sounded mysteriously like a growl.

I crouched down to meet her gaze straight on. "Promise me you won't try to leave this cave until I come back."

She snorted—or attempted to, anyway. "No wings."

Yes, I'd noticed that. Odd that she woke without her feathers. An indication that her body still required healing. "Promise me you'll stay here." Because I knew the lack of wings wouldn't stop her from trying. "I can't go out there while worrying about you, Evangeline." I caught her chin, forcing her to hold my gaze. "*You* are my weakness." She always had been, always would be.

She swallowed, her gaze misting. And finally nodded. "Promise."

"Good." I kissed her far too briefly and stood. "I'm only doing this for you, love."

Another partial snort. "Liar."

The edges of my lips twitched as I glanced back at her. "I never lie." I was only doing this for her, but that didn't mean I wouldn't enjoy it too. "You better be here when I return, Evangeline." I let the *or else* threat linger between us before stepping backward off the ledge and taking flight.

Time to play.

CHAPTER 10
BLOODY GOOD TIMES
HOSTED BY XAI

A Cyclops in Heaven.

That sounded like the brunt of a bad joke, but no one laughed as the giant, single-eyed beast stumbled through one of the three open portals. Direct links to Hell. That *never* happened and explained the odd explosions. Whoever had created these possessed a fucking death wish, one I intended to deliver when I found the culprit.

"Up!" my father shouted, pointing to a horde of winged demons taking to the sky.

Vultures.

I didn't even know they could exist outside of the underworld. They were much larger than their Earth equivalents, with wings as long as my own, humanoid bodies, and evil beaks that shot paralyzing venom at their prey.

Evangeline hated Slithers.

I hated Vultures.

Of course my father would task me with these assholes.

I grabbed a silver-tipped spear and a sword from the

armory and took to the sky. Seven total, all cawing in their creepy language at one another.

The only positive? They flew in a flock, giving me a single target.

I eyed their flight pattern and lined up my spear. At least they were predictable demons.

My spear shot through the sky with a precision that would have made Evangeline proud. Angry squawks littered the air as three of the Vultures met their fate, turning to ash midflight.

Their brethren turned on me, black ooze spitting from their beaks.

A shield would have been a good idea.

Next time.

My wings collapsed, sending me into a downward spiral as I avoided their venomous muck. A blade was far more elegant of a weapon. Mine glistened in the moonlight, the silver dying for some demon action.

Tucking and rolling to the side, I sprinted up behind the slowest of the Vultures and lopped off his head with a single swipe. His buddy—who turned at the wrong moment—was next.

Two left.

And they were furious.

More of that inky substance flew from their mouths, forcing me into another nosedive, this one coming far too close to one of the higher city buildings. I really hoped no one was on their balcony watching, because they'd get hit with a glob of Vulture poison.

The two demons stupidly followed me, just as before, allowing me to sail up behind them as I did their brothers. "Seriously, this wasn't even fun." I took them both out with two clean swipes of my sword and sighed. "So much for that party."

You're not missing much, I told Evangeline, uncertain if she could even hear me. From what Ashmedai said, our ability to communicate telepathically was rare and not a connection he'd ever seen. He hypothesized that it was our souls' way of reaching out to one another in moments of dire need. By that theory, Evangeline must have been close to death more than once at the hands of Kalida, thus creating our telepathic bond. A thought that had pissed me off on several occasions and only spurred me on more to find her.

Kalida would die.

Horribly.

But first, I had a few portals to see to.

I landed beside my father, his ancient chants music to my ears. An Archdemon—Bael—stood just inside the portal, his words rivaling those on our side, his silver-blue irises shining with foreign energy. A familiar woman with dark skin was beside him, her eyes closed as she helped him seal the portal from inside Hell's realm.

Johanna.

What was happening in this world? A member of the Divinity working with an Archdemon?

A low hiss had my sword reacting on instinct, slicing unerringly into a Guardian demon's heart. He collapsed into embers that I kicked away with my foot. Somehow he'd gotten through the ring of angels all protecting my father as he performed one of our oldest rituals—*The Sealing of Worlds.*

I stood at his back, ready to take on anyone else who dared try to interfere, but it was moot. My brethren had it handled, and from the excitement in their gazes, they were enjoying the fight.

Raphaela's words about letting the others in on the fun came back to me. Was that how they saw this? Something entertaining after an eternity of peace? Maybe they should visit Earth more often. The humans fell into wars once a century, it seemed.

A sizzling pop sent a shiver down my spine as the portal closed. The sparks in the distance confirmed the other two had shut as well. And around us was a sea of ash as the last of the demons wilted and died without their primary energy source.

Only Archdemons could stand in Heaven.

The others, even Demonic Lords, were too weak.

My father sagged, his knees giving out from the loss of strength. I caught him before he face-planted, my hands on his shoulders, holding him upright while granting him a moment to recover. He nodded his thanks, his eyes solid black from the energy exchange, his lips purple.

I possessed the same ability, knew what it required of my body to engage. It would take my father at least a night to recover, if not longer.

"Eve?" he asked, an unexpected touch of concern in his voice.

"She's fine," I replied, sensing her presence through our bonded souls. "Resting."

His throat worked. "That's just the beginning."

"How was that even possible?" I asked, gesturing with my chin toward the destroyed portal. Several angels stood around us, their expressions filled with curiosity as well.

"I don't know." He combed his fingers through his hair, expelling a breath. "It defies the balance."

Yes, speaking of balance... "Why was Johanna with Bael?"

My father merely shook his head. "Everything is changing." He sounded more exhausted than ever, as if his own power was falling by the wayside.

I helped him to his feet and frowned at his dragging wings. So unlike him.

"I need to rest," he replied softly. "We'll reconvene in the morning."

He didn't fly as he normally would; rather, he walked—slowly—through the circle and toward my waiting mother, just beyond the crowd. Concern etched her brow as she opened her arms to him, her ancient eyes meeting mine for a long moment.

Unspoken words passed between us.

Understanding.

A future she always knew would befall me.

She approved.

All broken bits of conversation that she somehow telegraphed into my mind before using her wings to lift herself and my father to take them home. She'd been waiting the whole time for him, knowing he would fall.

My mother, the Archangel of Destiny, always so oracular in her ways.

I shook my head, realizing that all the angels in the courtyard were awaiting further instruction—from me, the Son of Chaos.

They think of me as a leader.

The thought struck me hard in the chest, a weight I never wanted or expected falling over my shoulders. All those millennia on Earth protecting humanity had been an exercise in strength and understanding. My parents'—no, my *mother's*—way of preparing me for a prophesied future.

How do I know this?

Because I was also the Son of Fate.

I discarded the thought and focused on those around me. Enough insanity for one night. I had a mate to return to.

"We need more Sentries to stand guard overnight while the ancients heal." Because if my father was that exhausted, so were the other Archangels. "I recommend shifts of three hours each because you all need your rest as well. Something big is coming, and we're going to need all our strength." The words were mine but were spoken without my permission.

What was coming? And how did I know that?

I swallowed my confusion, not wanting the others to sense it, and forced my lips to twitch. "You all did well tonight. Good to see all that training has paid off."

That earned me a few chuckles and shouts of content, then the shoulder slapping started, which quickly grated at my patience. After the sixth or seventh one, I took a casual step back and took off into the night without another word.

They could manage themselves.

Besides, I wasn't their leader.

Not yet, anyway.

CHAPTER 11

I'M CRAVING A PLATE OF DEATH WITH A SIDE OF REVENGE, PLEASE

O*kay, Evangeline,* I told myself. *You can do this. Baby steps. One foot in front of the other.*

I'd spent the last hour trying to relearn how to walk without much success, but I was standing. While a reasonable start, I needed to do better.

Never had I felt so utterly *broken.* How long had I been unconscious? Days? Weeks? Months? It seemed like an inordinate amount of time had passed. Things *felt* different. Xai. Heaven. *Me.*

My back ached without my wings.

Where were they?

Why couldn't I sense them?

A tear tickled the corner of my eye, causing me to growl low in my throat.

I *hated* this. Despised feeling inadequate. Incomplete.

Kalida will die.

If Xai had killed her for me—

My knees buckled, sending me to my ass. Again.

"Fuck!" I shouted into the cave's abyss.

Frustration and horror trembled through my limbs, another treacherous tear leaking from my eye.

I wanted to beat someone and bawl at the same time. Kalida did this to me, had rendered me to this useless state.

"I will kill you," I vowed, thankful for my mostly healed voice. It showed progress.

Stand, I told myself. "Now," I added out loud.

Using the wall for support, I forced myself up and bit my lip at the ache shooting up my legs. Had I broken them? I couldn't remember. Everything post-Kalida was foggy. Something about Shadows...

Goose bumps pebbled along my arms at the thought, a shudder traversing my spine. Creepy little fuckers.

Stop thinking and walk.

Easier thought than done.

I took a shaky step and winced. Maybe if I had my wings for balance, this wouldn't be so difficult. A deep longing settled inside me as I wished yet again for my feathers.

And nothing.

My eyes closed. *What if my wings never come back?*

I swayed on my feet at the thought. My hands flew outward to help steady myself and connected with something hard on one side.

"Oh!" I jumped and my equilibrium went sideways. A pair of sturdy arms saved me from meeting the ground again.

"While I prefer this over your prone condition, you should be resting." Xai kissed my neck, his chest to my back. "Fuck, I've missed you." His hold tightened as he buried his face against my nape.

I tried to turn, but he didn't budge, his body very much in control of mine. "What happened, Xai? Were those portals?"

He sighed, his breath warm and welcome against my skin. "We don't know what or who created them yet, but the problem has been dealt with for tonight." He rotated me in his arms and captured my mouth in a kiss that bespoke of longing and pain. Every memory, every feeling, every desire was punctuated with his tongue against mine.

A relearning, I realized. He wanted to remind me of who we were to each other, how our bodies connected, where we belonged.

I wrapped my arms around his neck, threaded my fingers through his long, dark hair, and held on as he devoured me.

All my worries and concerns disappeared.

The agony rippling through my being vanished.

Only Xai mattered and the way his body felt pressed against mine.

"More," I demanded against his mouth.

He smiled. "I love that you think you're in charge here."

"I am."

"Mmm." His hands fell to my hips as he backed me up against the wall. "I told you I've missed you, and you didn't reciprocate, Evangeline. What should I do about that?"

I blinked up at him. "Make me show you how much I missed you?" I suggested.

"That would be contrary to you resting, love." His lips whispered over mine, brief enough to tease, long enough to prove his yearning. "No one knows you're awake yet. It's just us." He nuzzled my neck, his lips trailing over my collarbone. "But you're not healed enough for what I need to do to you."

I shivered under the promise of those dark words. "I won't break."

"I know," he whispered. "You never break, my strong,

103

resilient Evangeline." He kissed my jaw before hovering his mouth over mine again. "I almost lost you forever."

My heart skipped a beat at the torment etched into those words. "Xai..."

"You have no idea what it was like, searching for you and not knowing if I would ever find you in time. And seeing you beneath those Shadow demons." His forehead fell to mine, his grip on my hips tightening. "It nearly broke *me*. Do you understand that I would destroy everyone and everything for you? Had I lost you..." He swallowed roughly, tension rolling off him in waves. "I can't lose you."

I captured his face between my palms and forced him to meet my gaze. "You will never lose me, Xai. I'll always fight to find you." I smiled then, recalling some of the words whispered in my dreams. "And you'll always follow me anyway."

He didn't return my amusement, his midnight irises smoldering with unveiled emotion. "I could hear you in my head, Evangeline. Only briefly, and only when your soul called to mine, but I could *hear* your torment."

I stared at him. "That... that was real? I thought... I thought I had imagined your presence as a way to, I don't know, escape."

"It was your soul reaching out to mine to survive," he whispered. "It's rare and it's how I found you in the Shadow realm. The aura in your ring finally registered, but it was your soul that directed my path more than anything."

"Shadow fields?" I repeated, frowning. A shiver followed the words, plummeting me into blackness...

Dark beings feasting on my energy.
Sucking away every ounce of my strength.
Leaving me defenseless.
Alone.

Dead.

Forgotten.

Nowhere to go.

An endless pit of solitude and—

"Evangeline!" The shout brought me back, my watery eyes flashing up to a pair of simmering dark orbs. Worry crinkled his brow, his handsome face my favorite memory. I touched his jaw, his chin, his high cheekbones and ran my fingers through his thick, dark hair. The same color as the feathers at his back.

My dark angel.

"Why is your hair so long?" I asked softly, entranced by the length. He hadn't worn his hair this way in centuries.

His pupils dilated, a long breath escaping through his luscious lips. He seemed conflicted, if a little perplexed. "I spent a lot of time in Hell trying to find you and stopped caring about trivial things like my hair."

I continued fondling the strands. "I like it."

One side of his mouth quirked upward. "Then maybe I'll keep it."

"Okay," I whispered, unleashing the weight of my exhaustion in a yawn.

"You need rest, love."

I nodded. "Everything is so fuzzy." Even the last ten minutes or so. Or longer. I couldn't quite remember. There was something important to discuss. Maybe.

Another yawn.

We could discuss whatever it was after I slept a little more.

He lifted me off the ground, one arm under my knees, the other around my back. I snuggled into his shoulder, enjoying his strength and familiarity. "You smell like battle." One of my favorite scents. All woodsy and male, with just a hint of Xai beneath. "I like it."

He chuckled. "I'm going to enjoy bringing up this conversation in the morning."

"Why?"

"Because I have a feeling you won't remember it."

Why wouldn't I remember it? "Of course I will."

"We'll see." He kissed my forehead. "Get some sleep, love. I'll be here when you wake."

"Promise?" I didn't know why I said it, but part of me needed to be certain. *My soul missing her mate.*

"There's nowhere else in the realms I would rather be than by your side, Evangeline. I vow it." Another kiss, this one lulling me into a place of comfort and serenity I'd long lived without.

How many years?

Where was I again?

Hell?

Torture?

Shadows?

I trembled at the thought, my mind and body immediately averse to the word.

Sleep was what I needed—a far more pleasant notion. Maybe it would help me feel right again.

And bring me back my wings...

CHAPTER 12

DON'T TEMPT
ME, DARLING

"A residual shadowmare." Raphaela's expression turned thoughtful. "Like a nightmare, but of the Shadow realm. I imagine it's the first of many to come for Evangeline. The Shadow demons are not known for their mercy."

"She'll overcome it," my mother mused, her hazel eyes glistening with the knowledge of foresight.

I pushed away from the wall and went into the kitchen to grab a bottle of water. Both the matriarchs had tea—their favorite.

Evangeline's emotional break in the cave had frightened me, even more so when she appeared to be completely unaware of her behavior. It had taken me nearly ten minutes to silence her screams. Then she'd awoken and fixated on my hair.

"What about her wings?" I asked as I returned to the patio outside. Both females sat on backless chairs, their light-colored feathers brightening the balcony's otherwise dull appearance.

"She woke too early," Evangeline's mother replied. "Her body is still catching up to her mind."

"On the contrary, her timing was flawless." The Archangel of Destiny paused to sip her tea, drawing out her words in the way she always favored. "Her awakening placed Xai in his destined position. Had she slept, he would have missed his calling."

Oh, good. More cryptic tales from Mom. "What does that mean, Mother?"

She blinked at me. "What does what mean, darling?"

I shook my head, not interested in playing this game right now. "Never mind."

"You're almost ready," she added, ignoring me. "I'm so excited to *see* it. But oh." She glanced at the clock, her eyes brimming with too much knowledge. "We should be going, Rafa. Xai has plans."

My eyebrows rose. "I do?"

"You do." She set her empty teacup aside, her lips curling. "Or she does, anyway."

"Who does?"

"It's not polite to eavesdrop, by the way. But oh, I do believe you've been chastised for that before, yes?" She giggled to herself, her words making absolutely no sense whatsoever. "You'll find her in Alastor's realm in three Heaven days' time, my child. The Archdemon's not aware, so be kind or retaliation will be dire. But the Succubus deserves her fate." My mother blinked again in that eerie way, as if waking from some sort of dream. "Were we leaving, Rafa?"

Raphaela merely smiled, very used to my mother's strange ways. "We were, yes."

"Preparations," my mother replied, her voice holding an urgent undertone. "That's what we are to do. Follow me."

She stood and stepped off the balcony without a farewell, her opal-shaded feathers glistening in the early morning sunlight.

"I believe that's my cue." Raphaela smiled and patted me on the arm. "Evangeline chose well, Xai. Never doubt it."

"I don't." An arrogant reply, sure, but a truthful one. Evangeline was my mate. No one could ever deny that.

Her lips curled. "So much like your father, and yet, I see your mother in your eyes." She tilted her head to the side. "Try not to lose my daughter in Hell this time." She winked and followed my mother, leaving me shaking my head at them both.

I ran my fingers through my hair, bemused. "Crazy matriarchs."

"I've always thought you inherited your cryptic ways from your father, but I see clearly now that it was your mother." Evangeline stood in the entryway wearing absolutely nothing, her hip cocked against the doorjamb, one ankle crossed casually over the other.

My gaze traced every inch of her athletic form. She'd lost some weight during her captivity, but her angelic genetics were slowly reasserting themselves in the slight curve of her hips and supple weight of her breasts.

Gorgeous.

"How are you feeling?" I asked softly.

"Irritated," she replied, her blue eyes flaring.

I cocked a brow. "Irritated?"

"Yes." She stared me down. "I'm naked, Xai."

"I see that, Evangeline."

"Do something about it."

My lips twitched in amusement. "I would offer you my shirt, but I'm not wearing one." That seemed to be my constant state these days—bare feet, jeans, and shirtless. Oddly, I didn't miss my suits.

Her gaze narrowed. "You know that's not what I want."

I cocked my head to the side playfully. "What do you want, love?"

"Right now? To kill you."

"An entertaining proposition," I mused. "Try and maybe I'll reward you." It would serve as a dose of foreplay shrouded in a test of her strength. I refused to push her until I knew she could take it.

We didn't make love. We fucked. Hard.

I widened my stance and taunted her with a doubtful look.

Her resulting growl went straight to my groin. Coupled with her lack of clothes, well, my pants were suddenly feeling a bit tight.

"Having second thoughts, darling?" I took a step toward her. "Worried you might be out of practice?"

Her irises darkened to my favorite shade of sapphire, telegraphing her response before she moved. I caught her fist before it connected with my face and spun her in my arms with ease, her bare back meeting my chest. The heel kick she attempted at my shin had me lifting her from the ground in an impenetrable hug and elevating us into the sky.

She immediately stopped flailing, her heart picking up in rhythm.

"Xai…"

"Worried I'll drop you?" I asked against her ear. "Do you think it would force your wings to appear?" I would never do it, even if she said yes. But just the threat had her tensing.

She grabbed my forearms. "Don't."

"Afraid?"

Her escalating pulse answered for her. "Don't, Xai."

"If you're ready to fuck me, you're ready to fly." I loosened my grip just enough to drive the point home.

Her nails dug into my skin, drawing blood. "This isn't funny."

"Neither is you trying to seduce me when we both know you're nowhere near ready for me."

"So you're punishing me by reminding me that I don't have my wings?" she asked, her voice cracking. "As if I'm not already feeling on the cusp of breaking without them?"

Fuck. That hadn't been the point of this at all.

My flesh ripped from her grasp as I shifted her in my arms, forcing her to face me. Tears glistened in her eyes, breaking my heart.

"Oh, Evangeline." I touched my forehead to hers as I slowed our flight to a gliding pace among the clouds. "I'm sorry, love."

"It hurts," she said roughly, burying her head against my neck. "It hurts so fucking much that I need to forget, Xai. I can't. I need you to take it all away, the pain, the memories. I need you to love me. To show me I'm still good enough. To remind me who we are together. To promise me forever again. To prove I'm not as broken as I feel. Please, Xai. Please. I'm begging you. I'll—"

I threaded my fingers in her hair, yanked her head back, and silenced her with my mouth. It physically pained me to hear her so desperate, so *shattered*.

If she wanted to forget, I could give her that. I would give her anything she ever desired. She had to know that.

My tongue parted her lips, demanding entry, demanding she give me all her attention. No memories allowed. No darkness, except my personal brand. No thoughts of Hell, revenge, the powers shifting, none of it.

I drifted onto my back, gliding with the wind. Her arms circled my neck, her body melting into mine.

Fuck, I'd missed this.

Missed her.

Missed the air against my wings.

Fucking in the clouds...

"I love you," I told her. "You're my reason for being, Evangeline."

Tears cascaded down her cheeks as she returned my kiss with a passion that made my head spin. I let her take control, just for a moment, her tongue dueling heatedly with mine as she sought the reassurance she needed.

Then her palms were exploring my shoulders, my torso, my lower abs, the button securing my jeans.

It took all manner of restraint to grant her the power.

My zipper lowered, my cock springing free between us.

"More, Xai." Her teeth sunk into my lower lip. "You're holding back and it—"

I growled against her mouth, biting her back—harder —the taste of her blood hitting my tongue. "Wrap your legs around me, Evangeline."

She immediately complied, her wet heat meeting my shaft. My wings collapsed, sending us into a downward spiral. Her arms and legs tightened around me, her arousal mingling with fear.

Fragile or not, she wanted to forget. And I intended to deliver.

For her.

For us.

To make sure she never forgot who owned her, who owned me, who we were together.

"Mine," I growled, thrusting into her and up at the same time, taking her high into the sky while claiming her in the harshest of ways.

She cried out, her eyes glazing with tears for an entirely new reason, even as a grin curled her lips.

I kissed her then—truly kissed her—with everything in my being. Fucking her mouth as I did her body, pushing past every limit, owning every inch of her as she possessed my soul, and extinguishing whatever concerns she had about who she was to me.

"I love you," I repeated again and again and again. This time her tears were ones of bliss and happiness as she returned the words, her heart beating in time with mine as our bodies flourished in the clouds.

She shattered, but only in ecstasy, her orgasm chasing away all the residual torment and pain, her body convulsing in rapture as my name tumbled from her swollen lips.

"Another," I demanded, refusing to let her off that easily.

One arm remained wrapped around her lower back, holding her as my opposite hand drifted between us to her sensitive clit. She jerked, her body reacting from being stroked too soon, but I relentlessly continued, determined to see that look of euphoria on her face again before I joined her.

Her mouth opened on a scream, her head falling back as I drove into her harder. I used my wings to my advantage and took her the way I craved, the way she had required. And her chants told me she more than approved.

She clutched my shoulders, my biceps, my shoulders again, her body trembling against mine.

So close.

I removed my mouth from hers to bite her neck, my urge to mark her strong. "My mate," I growled. "Always. Forever. Mine." I bit her again as I pressed down harshly on her clit.

"Xai!" she screamed, fracturing around me, her walls clutching me so tightly I couldn't help but follow her into oblivion.

And fuck, it hurt in the best way, my balls tightening as I emptied myself deep inside her. Over and over, claiming every part of her, my soul marrying hers in a bond for eternity—again.

She shook violently, her forehead against my shoulder, and I realized with a start that she was crying.

"Evangeline," I whispered, concerned that I'd hurt her, damaged her in some way in my ferocity to reassert my dominion.

I scouted for a place to land, found one in a nearby field, and touched down while she bawled in my arms.

"Oh, darling..." This was why I didn't... shouldn't...

Her nails dug into my shoulders, her mouth finding mine as she kissed me through the sobs. I didn't understand, couldn't follow her logic.

What happened to you?

"Thank you," she whispered, kissing me harder. "Thank you."

I cradled her against me, returning her embrace despite my confusion.

"I love you," she continued. "God, Xai, I hate how much I love you, but I do. You're my reason, too. My mate. The one who always knows how to piece me back together." More kissing, more crying, more shaking. "I hate her, Xai. The things she did to me, she wanted to scar me, to ruin me so you wouldn't want me anymore, and I worried... I knew...

but I worried..." She paused, tears flooding her eyes. "God, I feel like such a fool for ever thinking..."

"Shh," I murmured, understanding now. She felt as if she betrayed me by believing such a thing possible. "Torture isn't just physical, darling. It's mental too." And clearly, Kalida had done more damage than either of us realized. "We'll heal together, sweetheart. It's what we do."

She buried her head in my neck again, her shoulders trembling violently as she cried, as she allowed herself to finally feel everything that had happened to her, in the safety of my arms.

Even angels as old as us needed to fall apart sometimes. What she had endured, most would never have survived. But my Evangeline was far from ordinary.

She was mine.

My purpose.

My eternity.

CHAPTER 13

I SEEM TO HAVE LOST TOUCH WITH HUMANITY

T he moon reflected off of Xai's feathers as he flew us back to his refuge, the home he claimed eons ago that no one else dared touch even in his absence. Silence had befallen the city, most of our kind settling in for the night while the Sentries guarded them in their sleep.

I laid my head against Xai's shoulder, exhausted both physically and mentally. He'd held me through my tears, fucked me again when I asked, and kissed me for what felt like hours.

His long hair tickled my cheek, causing me to smile despite my sleepy state. "I still don't want you to cut it."

He landed on his balcony with a chuckle, his ebony gaze finding mine. "We'll see if it suits the times when we return to Earth."

I considered that with a frown, my mind attempting to process the impossible. "What year is it down there?"

His shoulders lifted and fell. "I honestly have no idea at this point, but everything has changed. Again."

A reference to our last stay in Heaven.

I gasped. "Oh, shit, Gwen!" I hadn't spoken to her before everything happened, or even warned her that I was on a mission. Hadn't even thought about it.

What a great best friend I am.

"She knows where you are," Xai said as he lowered me to his bed and stretched out beside me. His pants were lost somewhere, likely never to be found. "Zebulon kept her informed during our search, and, according to your mother, Azrael has provided her with updates on your condition here."

"Zebulon?" I repeated warily, recalling Gwen's budding relationship with the Demonic Lord.

"They've grown close." Xai slid his arm beneath my shoulders and pulled me into him, his chest serving as the perfect pillow for my head. "He's good to her, from what I can tell. Zane, too."

I gaped at him. "What?"

"Yeah, I'll let her tell you that story," he replied, smirking. "We have something more important to discuss anyway."

"Do we?" I asked, not sure I agreed. *Gwen, Zeb, and Zane? The fuck?*

"Yes. Kalida."

The name wiped away all my thoughts of Gwen almost instantly, my need for revenge surfacing. "She needs to die."

"Yes, my mother said that as well. I suspect she was talking to you?"

I recalled her words from the balcony and nodded. "She knew I was standing just inside, listening."

"At least the eavesdropping comment makes more sense now."

Yeah, that subtle chastisement had been directed toward me. Not that I had cared. As much as I had wanted to see my mother, it was Xai I had desired most when I woke, and he hadn't been where I needed him. "Your mother said Kalida is in Alastor's realm, or will be."

"Yes, she doesn't normally give such obvious hints regarding the future, which tells me we needed her assistance to find Kalida."

I shook my head. "No, she was delivering a verdict of fate and requesting that death—me—handle the punishment." That much I understood by her statement. *"But the Succubus deserves her fate."*

"A death sentence," Xai said, catching on. "In less than three days' time."

"Which means I need to find my wings." And the rest of my strength.

He softly stroked my arm, his heart beating steadily beneath my ear. "Everyone is focused on the shifting of power, not on Kalida. She likely knows this, suggesting she's fallen into a state of comfort since no one is actively searching for her."

"No one?" I repeated, surprised. "Even Ashmedai?"

"Especially Ashmedai. He's preoccupied with protecting his lands and his people, as are the other Archdemons, even the Demonic Lords on Earth. Strange things are happening in the underworld, Evangeline, and no one knows the cause."

"Like the portals last night."

"Yes, exactly."

I considered that, my brow furrowing. "But weren't they like the ones Geier and Kalida created on Earth?"

Xai was silent a moment, his hand stilling on my arm. "Yes, but more powerful."

"Meaning someone has perfected them, which suits the timeline, right? How many thousands of years have passed in Hell since the incident on Earth?"

"You think Kalida is involved."

"How couldn't she be?" I asked. "Think about it. She and Geier started to create an army on Earth to take over her father's territory, and failed. But someone helped her escape, who I'm guessing has yet to be identified, indicating a level of power that supersedes or matches Ashmedai's. She also has a pet Nephilim who somehow masks her aura even when he's not by her side, and he thrives in Hell. Is all of that a coincidence?"

"You know how I feel about coincidences."

"Yes, it was a rhetorical question. We both know it's related." I went onto my elbow beside him, meeting his dark gaze. "Could it be another Archdemon tinkering with the balance?"

"It would require more power than that." He stroked my spine, his expression curious. "The Divinity is fracturing. I'm not sure what happened, but Johanna is in Hell with Bael, and I think Ezra is mated to a Halfling."

My eyebrows lifted. "Is any of that even allowed?"

"I'm not sure anyone is following the rules anymore." Amusement tugged at his lips. "Is it wrong that I approve?"

"No, it's very you." I leaned in to kiss him, my lips lingering against his. "Son of Chaos."

"And Fate," he added, his brow crinkling a little. "My mother seems to be indicating I have a new future path."

"I heard that," I whispered. "Something about your calling?"

He pinched my side. "You really were eavesdropping."

I shifted back with a snort. "You're one to talk."

He shrugged, unapologetic. "Regarding my mother, I'm

not clear on what she's predicting—as usual—but it sounds imminent. And..." He paused, his pupils contracting in an eerie way. "I sense it too, Evangeline."

I studied him, the mysterious thinning and expanding of his dark irises, the way he took on an almost faraway gleam as if searching for the thread of that elusive thought. "Your powers are strengthening, too."

He swallowed and nodded. "Yes, I think so. It would explain how I deepened our connection, how I survived the Shadow realm without so much as a scratch, how I managed to bend Ashmedai to my will, why the other angels seemed to be looking to me as a leader, how I sensed the portals last night before they formed..." He drifted off, his expression holding a twinge of concern.

"That's why I woke early," I realized. "You must have somehow triggered it when you felt the disturbance."

"No, that was your soul waking to the call of death." He said it with such confidence, as though he just *knew* it was true. And he didn't even notice it.

"You're the son of two Archangels. You've always favored chaos because it served you well in your role on Earth, but your mother's blood also lives within you. Maybe that ability is awakening."

"But why, after all these millennia?"

"Because it's almost time," I murmured. "Isn't that what your mother said?"

He considered it, his eyes taking on that faraway gleam again. "Yes. I just wish I knew what it meant."

"Something tells me we're going to find out, and soon."

He nodded, his fingers tracing my arm again as he pulled me back to him. "But we'll deal with Kalida first."

"Yes," I agreed. "And figure out how she's linked to all of

this." Because I felt it with every fiber of my being that she was involved. She had to be.

"That gives us two days to heal your soul and find your wings."

"Any idea where to start?" Because aside from my missing feathers, I felt almost normal. Almost.

"I do, actually." He flattened me beneath him, his lower body settling between my thighs. My breath came out in a shudder at the very intimate position and the feel of his hot, hard length against my tender flesh.

"Xai..."

"Evangeline," he returned, sliding into me. "You begged me to fuck you, did you not?"

I arched beneath him, a whimper escaping my lips that sounded mysteriously like an affirmative. I had begged him, would do it again if it meant another bout of pleasure and forgetting.

"Did you think we were done, darling?" He punctuated the question with a sharp thrust that had me sighing in content.

I loved him. This. Us.

My fingers threaded through his hair, pulling him down for a kiss that he denied with a grin against my lips.

"Beg me again, Evangeline."

I nipped at him instead. "Give me more."

He grinned. "So defiant."

"So arrogant."

He nuzzled my nose. "So perfect."

"So mine," I replied, tightening my grip in his hair.

"Forever, love."

"Show me." I licked his lower lip. "Promise me." Another trace of my tongue against his mouth, urging him to open. "Devour me." I dipped inside, humming in approval. "Take me." Those last two words were a breath against his mouth, my body shivering with want beneath him.

Electricity sizzled between us, his irises darkening to match his feathers. "Hold on to me, love."

I wrapped my arms around his neck and vowed, "I'll never let go."

CHAPTER 14

A QUICK GUIDE TO SEDUCING THE DAUGHTER OF DEATH: BUY HER SILVER TOYS

E vangeline balanced the sword with the ease of a practiced professional, her stance ready. "I still prefer knives."

"I know." I struck and she countered, her lithe form shifting with ease.

"And guns," she added while parrying my next move.

"I know," I repeated.

She arched a blonde brow. "Remind me again why we're doing this?"

"Because it's fun."

She gave me a dubious look and tossed her sword aside. "I prefer sparring."

I sighed, lowering my blade. "It's like you want to be killed."

Her fingers danced over the throwing daggers sheathed against her sides. "I'm still armed." Happiness glimmered in her gaze, confirming she approved of the items I'd gifted her this morning.

Most women wanted diamonds. My woman preferred silver knives. Not a problem in Heaven, where the substance existed in abundance. A little harder on Earth, but I managed.

"Then let's spar." I set my sword down beside her—much more gracefully—and widened my legs. "Show me what you can do, Evangeline." I laced doubt into my tone just to irk her. It worked.

Her eyes narrowed. "Gladly."

She moved faster than I expected, striking out with her foot instead of her palm and landing a hit to my thigh before sidestepping my counter. "That was actually good."

"You sound surprised."

"I am," I admitted. Her strength had certainly returned, and with it, her skill. Was it Heaven's atmosphere aiding her recovery? Her mother's healing power? Or was she, too, impacted by altering energies throughout the planes?

Another quick kick—this one I caught—followed by a punch that very nearly connected with my jaw. I dodged her second fist and returned one of my own that barely nicked her shoulder.

"More," I encouraged. Sparring with Evangeline was hotter than the best foreplay. It set my blood on fire and stirred an electricity between us that existed nowhere else.

We circled each other, striking, pulling back, kicking out, catching each other off guard, and moving until we were both breathing hard.

"I haven't seen you fight like this in eons," I whispered, awed.

"It feels good." She tried to knock me off balance with her leg, but I caught her and whirled her in my arms, placing her back to my front, my lips at her neck.

"You feel good." She attempted to elbow her way out of my hold, causing me to chuckle. "You may be quicker, love, but I'm definitely stronger."

More squirming until she finally conceded, her head falling back against my shoulder. "This isn't productive."

I pressed my hard cock into her backside. "I disagree."

"One-track mind," she groaned. "I need my wings, Xai."

It concerned me that they hadn't made their appearance, especially with her body being fully healed. Had the Shadow demons somehow damaged that part of her permanently? I hated that thought, despised the possibility, and refused to even voice it.

Rafaela would have sensed that, right? Evangeline, too?

"You're worried too," she said, sagging against me. "What if they don't come back?"

"They will." I rotated her in my arms and captured her face between my palms. "We just need to give it time."

"We don't have time," she argued. "She'll be in Alastor's realm today, Xai."

I sighed. Yes, two days had come and gone far too quickly. But there was an element to this that Evangeline seemed to be ignoring. "You don't need your wings in Hell."

She considered, her blue eyes holding mine. "But without them, I'm not at full health."

"You seem well enough to me," my mother said as she landed beside us.

"Hello, Mother," I murmured as Evangeline moved to my side, her arm around my lower back beneath my feathers.

"Should you not be headed to Ashmedai's realm right now?" my mother asked, ignoring greetings as usual.

"There are several paths, and I favor this one." Her uncanny eyes unfocused, refocused, and unfocused again, the patterns of the future shifting before her.

"The Succubus will say she knows, but she does not. Her fate lies in the hands of death. Consult with the

129

Daughter of War. She's powerful." My mother blinked, then smiled. "There, that'll do nicely. Have a safe trip, but do come back soon. We need you."

She took off in a flourish of color, her opal feathers glinting in the sunlight.

"Daughter of War?" Evangeline repeated. "Archangel Scion doesn't have a child."

An image flashed in my head, unexpected and unbidden, but utterly right. "Trudy."

Evangeline's gaze rose to mine, her eyebrows lifting. "What?"

"She's talking about Trudy." I had no idea how I knew that. The Nephilim looked nothing like her father, apart from maybe the cherubic facial features. "We need to go to Ashmedai's realm."

"But—"

"You're ready," I said, knowing exactly what Evangeline intended to say. "You're fighting better than you have in decades, and with my blood, you'll be strong enough to take on everyone in your path. And you'll have my wings, should you need them." Because I would be entering Hell in full Archangel mode.

Her blue irises contracted around her pupils, her expression one of respect rather than disquiet. "I trust you."

"I know."

"Even though you're an arrogant asshat."

My lips twitched. "I know."

"Good." She wrapped her arms around my neck. "Now give me some blood and we'll be on our way."

"Vampire."

"Chaotic Archangel," she returned.

I adored this woman more than breathing. "Kiss me."

"I thought you'd never ask."

"It wasn't a request," I corrected, my lips brushing hers. "Open." I sliced my tongue open with a sharp bite that stung, and slipped inside her waiting mouth. Instincts told me she wouldn't need much, which seemed contrary to past experience.

Our bond is strengthening.

Because we'd finally given in to it? Because of everything we'd been through together of late? Because of the changes in Hell rising to Heaven? All of the above?

Her moan against my mouth brought me back to her, to us, to our embrace. I deepened our kiss, forcing more of my essence into her, encasing her in my protection by filling her with Chaos's bloodline. She would be able to move about Hell as freely as I did, at least temporarily. I would give her more the second I sensed her weakening, and together, we would find Kalida and bring her to justice.

I traced the seam of her mouth with my tongue, loving the taste of her. "Ready?" I asked softly.

She nodded. "I have my knives."

I retrieved my favorite sword, sheathed it against my hip, and grabbed a few throwing stars from the weapons table. It seemed my mother had found us in the right location at the right time.

Fate.

I grasped Evangeline by the waist, aligning her body with mine. "Hold on."

She wrapped her arms around my neck and captured my gaze. "As if I could ever let you go."

"It's true," I told her, smirking. "If you tried, I'd just follow you."

"Stalker," she teased.

"Possessive," I corrected, engaging my shields and plummeting us toward the underworld.

A map of where I wanted to go formed in my thoughts, helping me hone in on the current location for Ashmedai's realm. The worlds of Hell were constantly shifting, making this sort of travel difficult. It took focus, control, and accuracy.

Evangeline said nothing, her arms strong around me, her legs brushing mine. Had it not required all my attention to navigate, I would have kissed her. Alas, arriving safely mattered most.

Our feet touched down near the steps of Ashmedai's building, my wings cocooning our forms as Evangeline gathered her bearings.

"You okay, love?"

She swallowed. "I feel different." Her lids rose to showcase a pair of dazzling blue eyes—as dark as the sapphire on her ring. Her limbs began to tremble, her lips parting on a sharp gasp.

"What is it?" I demanded, my hands on her hips, holding her steady as convulsions shook her from head to toe.

Electricity crackled between us, *through* us.

Evangeline's arms fell from my neck, her hands fisting at her sides as she tossed her head back. Euphoria sailed through our bond, her mouth curling into the most beautiful of grins.

Light erupted as her wings ripped through her back, her violet feathers a gorgeous contrast to my black ones.

A joyous laugh tumbled out of her, causing my lips to twitch.

"Always so defiant," I murmured, nuzzling her throat. "You're not supposed to have wings in Hell." Only Archangels possessed that ability outside of Heaven, but of course Evangeline found a way to defy reason.

Her lips touched mine, her elation washing over us both.

Demonic auras surrounded us, their tension palpable.

I ignored them and returned Evangeline's kiss, my tongue mating with hers in time's oldest dance. She smiled against me, her arms circling my waist, her breasts against my bare chest. Fortunately, she'd worn a shirt with a low back today for our sparring, just in case her wings returned.

The clearing of a throat by an impatient Archdemon had me grinning against Evangeline's lips. "I believe Ashmedai is ready for us."

She didn't appear apologetic in the slightest. "Oh? Then I suppose we should address him."

I pulled my wings to my back with a chuckle as she did the same.

Ashmedai stood leaning against the stair railing with Trudy at his side. Interesting how she always seemed to be with him, and again, they both wore matching warrior leather.

Mates, a foreign part of my mind whispered.

Impossible, I replied.

The Archdemon arched a brow. "Are you here to gossip or to help us?"

An interesting reaction to my thoughts. "That depends on what you need help with," I replied. "My cryptic mother sent us, something about different paths."

Ashmedai snorted. "Fucking Fate." He turned, his navy wings vivid beneath the blue-tinted sun. "Follow us."

Trudy moved with him without a word of greeting, her steps confident.

"How long has she been down here?" Evangeline whispered as we started after them.

"Several thousand years," Trudy replied, her sanguine

voice filled with age and experience. "But time passes strangely when you frequently venture between the planes."

Ashmedai placed his palm at the small of her back, and she moved closer to his side. Evangeline grabbed my forearm, the only indication that she'd noticed and a subtle hint that we would be discussing this later.

Maybe they really had mated.

We entered the entertainment hall of Ashmedai's opulent palace and continued down an ornately decorated corridor to what appeared to be a war room of sorts. Maps littered one long wall, surveillance feeds played across from it, and a tactical drawing took up another space.

The demons had been busy.

I studied the familiar realms, compared them to the ones in my mind, and realized the majority of these were a prediction of the future with the shift incorporated. Varying colors seemed to indicate sides, and their counterparts were situated in the various territories of Earth. Zebulon and Ashmedai shared the same shade, confirming them as allies.

Evangeline studied all the drawings with a trained expression, her millennia of experience marking her as prepared for such an outcome. "A demonic war," she said flatly. "But who are the beings in red?"

"Enigmas," Ashmedai replied. "Beings rising to power via unknown means and draining the resources from others."

She touched a gray marker. "And the gray?"

"The drained resources," Trudy said, joining her at the board. "The Archdemons are losing power and dying, as are their constituents. Those in blue—like Ashmedai—have yet to be affected."

"Because they acquired their own sources of power," I said, impressed. "That's why you wanted Trudy, why Bael has Johanna, and let me guess, Alastor has someone of interest too?" He was a solid blue on the chart, indicating his thriving power. "You've all tapped into the balance to save yourselves."

Ashmedai merely shrugged. "We do what is necessary to survive."

Trudy snorted. "Yes, it's been such a hardship on you."

Those purple eyes of his twinkled. "Extremely hard, yes."

The Nephilim—or whatever she was now—narrowed her gaze. "Careful, Ash. I know all your weaknesses."

"Isn't that what makes it more fun?" he asked, cocking his head to the side. He winked at her before focusing on me. "How are your elders?"

"Healing," I replied. "Trudy's warning granted us with enough time to prepare, though I think most are still reeling from the breach. Even with the foresight and preparation, no one thought it would actually happen."

"It's going to happen again, and soon." Trudy pointed to a red area of Hell. "There are troops amassing here, and it's not to start a battle in Hell."

"So either Earth or Heaven," I murmured, studying the numbers listed on the tactical map. "That's a lot of demons."

"Yes," she agreed. "Led by powerful entities without names."

"Because you don't recognize them?" I guessed.

"Because we can't identify them." Ashmedai folded his arms. "From what we've gathered, they're minor demons who have somehow accumulated enough power to cloak themselves."

"Similar to Kalida," Evangeline put in, her brow furrowing. "She masks her aura because of Grant—a Nephilim. But he's nowhere near strong enough to conceal that many demons."

Ashmedai shook his head. "Kalida is a ghost. While I see the obvious connection, it's very unlikely she's involved."

"He's right." Trudy shuffled through some papers—what appeared to be more maps and surveillance documents—on a nearby desk and picked a grainy photograph to hand to Evangeline. "That's the last image we have of her on record. It's over seven hundred Hell years old, and it was taken on Earth."

Evangeline studied the photograph with a frown. "So you just gave up trying to find her?"

Trudy narrowed her hazel eyes. "We've had more important matters to handle, in case you haven't noticed."

"Which is a yes, then. You've ignored your most obvious link." Evangeline set the photo down with a shake of her head. "Those portals the other night were created by the same magic Geier and Kalida used on Earth, just stronger. That can't be a coincidence."

"Geier is dead," Ashmedai informed. "And Kalida is too weak to be behind any of this."

I cocked a brow. "He's dead?" Last I knew, the former Demonic Lord was alive and in custody.

"Tru," Ashmedai said, a devious glint in his gaze as he glanced at her.

"He pissed me off," she muttered. "So I stabbed him with a silver blade."

"After cutting off his head," Ashmedai added. "It was glorious, Xai. You would have enjoyed it."

As much as I wanted to disagree, I couldn't.

"You've really come into your own," Evangeline

marveled, pride shining from her gaze. "I'm sorry I missed so much of it, that it had to happen here. I feel as if I failed you."

Trudy smiled, the first sign of her youth shining through. "I've never blamed you, Eve. Or Xai."

"Notice how I'm not on that list," Ashmedai mused.

"You know exactly why you're not on that list," she retorted, her smile fading into a glower underlined in adoration.

Definitely mates.

How that happened, I had no idea, but it had to be one hell of a story.

"How long have you known she was Scion's daughter?" I asked, my question for Ashmedai.

"From the moment I first read her file. There was no other bloodline appropriate for the favored protégé of Death." He brushed his knuckles down her arm. "I'm surprised you didn't figure it out when she delivered the warning in Heaven. Who else could possess such strategic foresight, but the Daughter of War?"

"That's why your mom sent us here first." Evangeline stepped into my side, her wings brushing mine. "To consult with Trudy."

"It's Tru." The former Nephilim sounded partly amused, partly irritated. "I haven't gone by Trudy for a very long time, and I'm pretty sure I've corrected both of you on several occasions now."

Evangeline gave her a sad smile. "You'll be Trudy to us for a while longer. You were just a small girl only months ago, or maybe a few years ago. Honestly, my concept of time is a bit muddled at the moment."

As was mine. But one mission remained clear. "On the

subject of time, we are slowly running out of it if we have any hope of catching Kalida."

Evangeline straightened, her shoulders tensing. "Yes. The Archangel of Destiny provided us with a location but wanted us to stop here first."

"You know where Kalida is hiding?" Trudy sounded intrigued, while Ashmedai appeared bored.

Funny how he'd been the one to start all of this and now he no longer cared. *Some may think you orchestrated it to capture Trudy.*

His lips twitched. "Fate works mysteriously, wouldn't you say?"

The women glanced at him, confused, while my gaze narrowed. "You still owe Evangeline a wound, Ashmedai. Don't think I've forgotten."

"Of course." He sounded far too amused for a male about to be stabbed. "But might I suggest we find Kalida first? Unless you want me out of commission for the fight?"

Evangeline gaped between us. "What are you talking about?"

"Ash agreed to let you stab him without retaliation," Trudy explained softly. "Back when you were missing, I mean."

Her eyebrows lifted. "Why?"

"Because Xai required it," Ashmedai said with a grin. "He blamed me for Kalida taking you."

She seemed to consider that, her gaze darkening. "Actually, yes, *you* were the one who wanted us to find her in the first place." Her attention shifted to me and back to him. "Wait—"

Trudy grabbed Evangeline's arm. "Okay, before we travel down Blame Ash Road—which is one of my favorites, by the way—could you give me Kalida's location so I can start strategizing?"

Evangeline shook her head, bemused and clearly torn between priorities—finding Kalida or stabbing Ashmedai. Her need for revenge won in the end, as she pointed at the map. "Alastor's realm. That's all we know."

"Alastor?" Ashmedai and Trudy asked at once. "That's impossible," the Archdemon added. "He would never allow it."

"Unless he doesn't know." Trudy tapped her chin. "He has one of the remaining Earth portals. Could she have slipped through undetected?"

"Is that what you would do?" he countered. I immediately recognized what he was doing—pushing his mate to think for herself, granting her independence and strength with a simple nudge.

I begrudgingly approved since I often performed the same tactic with Evangeline. She didn't need my confirmation, just my support and my occasional offhanded insult to encourage her to prove me wrong. I preferred the challenge, as did she, which was why she frequently did the same to me.

"Yes." Trudy pointed to an entrance. "Here. But the real question is, why would she venture into Alastor's realm when she could hide in so many other areas of Hell without the potential for detection?"

"Because Alastor is the Archdemon of Pestilence, with a direct portal to Earth," Evangeline whispered, her face paling. "Taking over his realm would give those in power the key to destroying Earth."

"Which is why his realm is the most heavily guarded right now," Ashmedai put in, frowning. "He's ready for that attack."

"Unless he can't see the threat coming," Evangeline said. "Regardless, we need to go to Alastor's realm. Now."

"Ashmedai can't," Trudy said, grasping his wrist. "His realm requires his presence for protection. But I can go with you."

He growled low in denial. "Absolutely not."

She stared up at him, undisturbed by the possessive energy rolling off him. "We have an agreement, Ash."

He held her gaze for a long moment, some sort of silent exchange of wills bouncing between them. Then he grabbed her and kissed her with such ferocity that I almost smiled. It reminded me of myself with Evangeline, and the spark in her gaze as she glanced up at me said she felt the same. I reached out to squeeze her hand, and she returned the gesture.

Trudy broke away from Ashmedai, her chest heaving from the exertion. "Don't. Do. That."

He merely smirked. "I love when you chastise me, princess."

She grunted in irritation and ran her fingers through her hair before smoothing out her clothes. "We should go. I'll find a Portal Dweller."

Good. That would help me save energy, and I suspected it would be needed.

CHAPTER 15

CONGRATULATIONS! YOU'VE JUST BEEN PROMOTED TO MY KILL-ON-SIGHT LIST!

The lack of blue overcast in Alastor's realm was a welcome change, but I could do without the heat. "It's like standing inside a furnace," I muttered.

Xai snorted. "Summer in Hell."

"I prefer winter." In the underworld, anyway.

"Likewise." His feathers touched mine, something he'd done constantly since my wings returned. I stroked him back, content at his side as we waited for Alastor to greet us. Trudy had called ahead, saying she had an acquaintance in his court.

I still couldn't wrap my head around her living in Hell, and apparently as Ashmedai's mate. All the surviving Archdemons had procured heavenly ties of some sort, and even some of the Archangels had tied themselves to members of Hell.

How could so much change in such a brief time? Sure, a few thousand years had passed in the underworld, but it had been only a decade or so on Earth, and not even two weeks in Heaven. For all this to crumble seemed impossible. Contrived. *Planned*.

"They'll see you now," a female voice chimed from beneath a dark blue robe.

"*They*?" I repeated.

Xai shrugged. "Perhaps Alastor has taken a mate?"

"Oh, don't call Lucía that unless you want to piss her off," Trudy warned, leading the way. "She and Alastor do not get along."

"Lucía, as in, from the Divinity?" Xai asked, sounding as flabbergasted as I felt.

"The very one." Trudy must have missed our shocked expressions, because she followed the blue-robed minion without another word.

"Everything is out of balance," I whispered.

"Or rebalancing," Xai mused, his palm against my lower back. "We were due for change."

True. It'd been several millennia since Heaven and Hell last experienced a realignment. Earth had been at the core with the creation of the Divinity, which appeared to have been disbanded.

My eyebrows rose at finding Alastor and Lucía seated on dual thrones, wearing evening attire as if attending some fancy gala. Alastor's suit was specially designed to accommodate his dark brown wings, as was his backless chair.

Lucía, being a daughter of an Archangel and an Archdemon, never possessed feathers. A consequence of a sort for her parents defying the balance by creating her. But while she lacked wings, she certainly possessed power, and it shone brightly in her multicolored eyes.

"Son of Chaos, Daughter of Death," she greeted formally. "Are you here about the disturbance?"

Alastor snorted, his gorgeous face twisting with annoyance. "You just sent off the call, Lucía. Not even Heaven works that quickly."

"You speak of things you do not understand," she returned, her voice holding an edge. "Son of Chaos is also Son of Fate, and I am guessing his mother sent him. Am I wrong?" Her eerie eyes went to Xai, seeking confirmation.

"If the disturbance you speak of was a perimeter breach, then yes," he replied smoothly.

"Excellent." She looked to Alastor, completely unfazed by his perfect cheekbones, chiseled jaw, and handsome features. I mean, I preferred Xai, but even I could admit the Archdemon was beautiful. They all were. "As I've said before," she murmured, "Heaven is superior in all ways."

"Do you see what I'm forced to live with daily?" he asked, gesturing to her with a lazy wave of his hand. "She's impossible. Please take her with you."

Lucía pursed her lips and refocused on us. "For every one hundred years in Hell, I am allowed one hour in Heaven. You would think my upholding his realm and protecting his people would be worthy of gratitude, but instead, I am stuck babysitting an Archdemon who prefers to behave like a child."

Alastor chuckled. "Nothing childlike about me, sweetheart."

She glanced upward, her patience clearly thinning. "The disturbance you seek is two blocks north." She rattled off a few details, including an address of a sort that only those in Hell would understand. "Take some guards with you. She's oozing malice."

"No guards required." Alastor stood and fastened the solitary button of his charcoal-gray suit jacket. "I'll join them."

"Don't be ridiculous. You'll stay here and let them

handle it." Lucía's tone brooked no argument, not that Alastor appeared to care. If anything, he seemed amused by the prospect of defying her.

"Finding and killing a rogue demon with them sounds far more exciting than another moment in your company, *Your Highness*." He mock-bowed with the sarcastic twist of his words and joined our party.

Trudy had stood off to the side the entire time with a smirk on her face, clearly used to the banter between Alastor and Lucía.

My expression likely held a touch of bewilderment, because wow. Whoever orchestrated this arrangement clearly hated one or both parties involved. Lucía and Alastor could not be any more different in their temperaments and personalities.

"Fine," Lucía replied. "I could use the peace and quiet."

"Oh, trust me, darling, so could I." He gave her a wave and led the way.

"Thank you for making the call," Xai said to Lucía, his head tilted in slight reverence. "We'll handle it."

"You're most welcome," she replied in that primly proper way of hers. "And feel free to kill Alastor in the process. On accident, of course."

"I heard that," the Archdemon called from the exit.

"I had hoped you would," she returned, her lips curling in triumph. "Just trying to prolong the silence, *darling*."

"And I've given you several ideas on how to do that," he tossed back at her. "Perhaps you should consider them while I'm away."

Crimson crept up her neck as she narrowed her gaze. "*Never*."

"I love when you lie," he replied, winking. "Shall we?"

he asked the rest of us, his hand already on the door handle. "I'm eager to kill something."

"Yes," I said. "Me too."

He smiled. "Daughter of Death, how I approve."

Xai's palm tensed against my lower back, his demeanor otherwise calm. "You mentioned leading the way?" he prompted, just a hint of a bite to his tone.

Alastor chuckled. "Possessive, as you should be. And yes, follow me." His dark chocolate wings touched the floor as he walked, an indication that, despite the elegant attire, he preferred casual environments.

"Bye, Lucía," Trudy called over her shoulder. "I'll reach out to have lunch soon."

"Please do. I could use the break!"

Trudy chuckled as she followed at my back, closing the door to the chambers behind us. "You're friends?" I asked, surprised.

"Somewhat, yeah. We bond over frustrating Archdemons," she murmured, a smile in her voice.

Alastor scoffed at that, his annoyance palpable. "I'm considering this a vacation. There will be no talk of the Divinity or that thing living in my palace, yes?"

"A vacation," I mused. "Shrouded in blood."

"And see, I knew I liked you." He winked over his shoulder, which stirred a low growl from Xai. "Innocent flirting, Son of Chaos. Promise."

"Try not flirting," he replied darkly.

Alastor shrugged. "You clearly know nothing about me." He opened the side exit, where a horde of blue-cloaked demons boasting Alastor's seal was waiting.

"She's going to see us coming," I muttered low, mostly to Xai.

"I have an idea for that," Trudy replied softly. "Alastor?" she asked, louder.

"Yes, sweetheart?" he asked, turning to face her with a wicked grin meant to strip women of their common sense. "How can I help you?"

She—like Lucía—appeared unfazed, probably because Ashmedai used the same tactics. "I'd like to discuss strategy. We have Kalida's location, but we need to be smart about this, as she has a penchant for escaping."

He leaned against the doorway. "I'm listening."

Excitement brightened her expression as she dove into an attack plan that was impressive and detailed and put me exactly where I wanted to be—as the one destined to kill Kalida.

"Seemed fair, considering," Trudy added after noting that part.

"I agree," Xai murmured, his thumb tracing the top of my jeans at the base of my spine. "But I will be with her."

Trudy nodded and continued with two backup plans, just in case our original didn't work, and finally looked to Alastor for approval. He merely shrugged. "I usually prefer a slower death involving disease, but I'll settle for a bloody one."

"You can infect Grant with something," I offered. "As a gift for your assistance?"

He smiled. "Would you be watching?"

"Yes." My soul required the vengeance associated with the Nephilim's death. If it was painful? All the better.

"Then it's a date." He grinned at my scowling dark angel. "You're welcome to join us. I don't mind."

Xai didn't reply, merely slid his palm down to cup my ass and pull me closer to him. I laid my head against him, reciprocating the display of ownership.

Trudy cleared her throat. "I suggest we go before we miss our chance."

The notion of Kalida escaping sent flames through my veins, heating me to my very core with the need to seek revenge. Her black spirit had tainted the lives of others, my own included, and for that, she would die. Justice *needed* to be served.

"Go," Xai whispered. "I'll follow."

I didn't respond, my feet already moving toward my target, my soul craving retribution. Being the Daughter of Death didn't mean I enjoyed killing. It meant I harbored the responsibility of delivering judgment to those who had wronged others, and Kalida was at the top of my list.

It's time.

Yes.

Her sentence must be served.

Yes.

Find her. Find her now.

Yes.

I jogged in the direction Lucía had described, growing more certain with every step that I'd located my mark. My senses stretched, seeking her aura and coming up empty.

Grant.

Punishment is required.

I know.

Xai's feet were silent behind me, but I felt his presence like a brand against my heart. *Mine in all ways.* I'd hardly noticed being in Hell, my body feeling more alive and stronger than I ever remembered it feeling. No aches, no weakness, just solid power and energy thriving inside of me.

Whether from my link to Xai or something else, I didn't know. And I didn't have time to ponder it now.

The building Lucía detailed stood a dozen feet before me. Nothing out of the ordinary, just a standard two-story home with stucco siding and a glistening black roof. I leapt into the air with a beat of my wings and landed quietly on top of the house, just as we decided. Xai dropped beside me, his glorious feathers blending with our surroundings, his gaze vigilant.

I listened for signs of life, conversation, anything to indicate Kalida was still inside.

Nothing.

I crept forward, eyeing the second-floor balcony and the billowy curtains suggesting someone had left the sliding door open.

Too easy.

A trap.

Xai seemed to agree, his head giving a shake in the negative.

The others around us were all getting into their positions—Trudy climbing the roof of the home across from us, a pistol I hadn't noticed before in her hand. Alastor had taken to the sky with three of his Royal Guard members, pretending to be out for an afternoon flight. Two other Guards were in similar locations to Trudy, everyone preparing to ambush Kalida and whoever kept her company.

I considered the scene, our backup, the weapons we carried, and smirked.

Yeah. Why bother with a sneak attack, really, when we clearly had the bitch outnumbered?

We could have some fun.

Xai arched a brow. *What do you have in mind, love?* he seemed to ask.

I smiled and nodded with my head. *Follow me.* I jumped off the building and landed in the sand covered street.

The home had no obvious entry point aside from the high windows—windows that I suspected weren't actually as open as they appeared. We were in Hell, after all.

Where's the door? I wondered, studying every detail of the brown exterior. The varying patterns etched into the siding flowed seamlessly into one another, except for the spot on the corner.

I gestured to it with my eyes and Xai grinned. *Let's go.*

Trudy had suggested an ambush. While I approved, I didn't need the backup. Death craved vengeance and I would deliver.

I moved with care over the ground, cognizant of potential traps. A tiny scrap of misshapen rock in the ground two feet before the entry had me nearly laughing.

A sound bomb, I told Xai with my glance.

He looked about as unimpressed as I felt.

Seriously, Kalida could do better. It was almost as if she wanted to be discovered. And unless she had a gun pointed and ready inside, she stood no chance.

I examined the wall pattern, searching for the trigger. *Gotcha.* I held my fingers out in a countdown. On one, I palmed a blade and kicked the spot as hard as I could.

The entry formed, sucking me inside with Xai at my heels. It knocked me off-kilter just long enough for someone to leap up from the living area with a shout. Male, not female, but I didn't care. My knife landed unerringly in his head, ceasing his yelling.

I stepped inside, another weapon already sliding into my hand.

Someone started down the stairs and froze upon

catching sight of me in the entry. Starless eyes, black hair, scarred face.

Kalida.

I smiled. "Honey, I'm home."

She scrambled forward, her arm lifting, a pistol in her hand.

I didn't hesitate, my knife already sailing through the air to meet her wrist. The force of it knocked her backward, my blade going straight through her bone to pin her against the ground.

"Beautiful," Xai praised, pleasure evident in his tone.

"Child's play," I replied. But it really was a spectacular throw, especially with the way it held my target captive. Kalida could extricate herself by tugging out the knife, but the pure silver handle made that particularly difficult for a demon.

"Miss me?" I asked darkly.

She growled, her free hand going to her jeans pocket.

I tsked, palmed another blade, and sent it into her shoulder, effectively slicing her tendons.

She screamed in agony, some demonic word falling from her lips.

"I'm sorry." I cocked my head to the side. "Did that hurt?"

A gurgling reply was my answer.

My lips twitched. "Good."

"Darling." Xai held out his sword, hilt first. "Can you use this?"

I cocked a brow at him. "Seriously?"

"Humor me."

I sighed, accepting his oversized weapon. "This is only because I love you."

Anticipation swirled in his midnight irises. "Then make it bloody."

That I could do.

I approached her trapped form, my steps light, my soul singing with the need for justice. "While I would love to know more about your relationship with Grant and how you've used him to conceal yourself, your death matters more, Kalida."

No way in hell was I going to draw this out and give her a chance to escape.

Not again.

And fuck asking questions.

Fuck everything.

I just wanted her dead.

I nudged her chin with the sharp edge of the sword, needing to see her eyes. "Thank you, Kalida," I murmured. "For trying to break me." I knelt beside her, holding her horrified gaze. "Because of you, I've never been stronger."

She called out again, her demonic words gibberish as her expression morphed into the agony of betrayal. Had she really expected Grant to be strong enough to save her? Not fucking likely.

It's time.

My soul ached, begging me to finish this, to rid the universe of Kalida's black existence *now*, desiring the end to her cruel ways.

Kalida had done enough.

She needed to disappear.

"Goodbye, Kalida," I whispered, the lethal point hovering just over her heart as I stood. "May you rest in eternal Hell."

I applied more pressure than necessary, forcing the sword through her heart and into the floor beneath her. A sharp exhale shuddered from her lips, her body processing the silver in her heart and pumping it through her veins.

Xai said nothing as I watched her life wither away.

Did nothing as her eyes rolled into the back of her head.

And smiled as her remains turned to ash.

Her spirit lifted, that intoxicating energy turning toward me and joining the Soul of Death, just as all those who came before her. I closed my eyes, welcoming her home, morphing her negativity into positivity in an instant, and feeling peace settle in the atmosphere around us.

Gone.

Destroyed.

Clean.

Her sentence delivered.

"You needed it to be quick," Xai murmured, his movements whispering around me.

I nodded.

"The others will be disappointed, but I'm glad it's done, even if she deserved a far harsher fate," he said, the clink of metal indicating his retrieval of our weapons.

"Justice," I managed in a whisper, my eyes still closed as my soul continued to process Kalida's demise. "Justice is served."

A slow clap sounded from above, followed by the creaking of stairs as a being I hadn't seen in ages slowly descended, his gaze aged and cold.

Dariel.

The Archangel of Concealment.

CHAPTER 16

TIME FOR CHAOS TO COME OUT AND PLAY

"The Archangel of Destiny always did enjoy her meddling," Dariel murmured as he reached the bottom step. "Not that I'm concerned. Kalida had reached the end of her usefulness long ago, but Grant insisted on keeping her."

I moved to Evangeline's side, her body tense in surprise. "Dariel," I greeted flatly.

"Xai," he returned, his voice void of emotion.

"When Ashmedai suggested you might be Grant's patriarch, I said you'd be offended by the insinuation. Fascinating that he was right." I hadn't thought much of it at the time. Now I realized my error. "It's good to put a face with the orchestrator of this madness, but you're not working alone."

"I'm not," he agreed, his lips twitching. "Perhaps you should ask your mother for more names? Oh, but that's only if she survives."

My eyebrow lifted. "Is that a threat?"

"More like an indication of current events," he replied, his feathers flaring to blend in with the brown texture around him. Not many possessed the ability to change their appearance, but as the Archangel of Concealment, he could. In all ways. "See, I knew she would send you here," he continued. "Actually, I guaranteed it."

An unsettling feeling stirred inside of me, one of foreboding.

"Have a safe trip, but do come back soon. We need you."

What had my mother seen intertwined into those paths?

"You feel it, don't you?" Dariel took a final step, landing on the ground before us with a finality that shook my being. "Heaven falling. Those portals before were just a test of strength, and they served as a way to weaken the strongest of our kind. Now they stand no chance, not with their forces divided."

Because you're not the only one who has chosen this path. The thought came from that foreign place inside of me that had only recently awakened. *There are more traitors in Heaven.*

"Why choose this path, Dariel?" I asked, curious rather than afraid. My instincts told me this was where I needed to be, and I trusted them.

"Are you not bored by the peaceful divide?" he countered. "Wouldn't it be more fun to manage our own territories on Earth? Obtain our own mortal subjects? Why are demons the only ones allowed to have all the fun?"

I stared at him. "You believe consorting with humans to be fun?"

He shrugged. "They die so often that I'll have a constant supply of new toys. What isn't enjoyable about that?"

Age insanity, I realized. Dariel had gone mad with time. It happened—not often—when the most ancient among us forgot our core values and favored more lethal pastimes instead.

"You've lost your fucking mind," Evangeline said, her body tense with the need for retaliation. "Without the balance, Heaven will be destroyed."

His lips curled. "I know."

"He doesn't care." I tilted my head, eyeing him. "He wants Heaven to Fall, thus changing Earth for eternity. But what of Hell?"

"What about it?" he asked with a disdainful look around. "It's already crumbling from the imbalance. It's an inferior realm. Let it destroy itself."

"The demons will move to Earth." Evangeline's tone suggested her impatience with this conversation, and the blade twirling between her fingers confirmed her proposed solution.

But a knife wouldn't take down Dariel.

Only an Archangel of equal or greater strength could destroy him, but a lot of beings would be destroyed in the process, including—potentially—her.

Which was why I didn't react, merely stood with my feet braced, ready to protect her if necessary, but otherwise not engaging the clearly mad Archangel before me. I needed a better plan first.

"Not if all the portals and Portal Dwellers are destroyed," Dariel replied conversationally. "Why do you think I'm here, Evangeline?"

"Because you're insane and craving death?" she suggested sweetly.

"Alastor's portal," I answered before he could reply to her sarcasm. "You're here to destroy it." It served as the primary gateway between Hell and Earth, heavily guarded on both sides. Demons with proper clearance were granted passage, and it was the only portal in existence that Heaven allowed to remain open at all times.

Of course, Dariel wished to destroy the bridge. It would only further fracture the delicate balance between our worlds.

He gazed at me with renewed interest. "I've always thought you were more intelligent than Mietek and never understood why he relegated you to protect humanity when you so clearly were born with a far greater purpose." He sounded impressed, an emotion we did not share. "Seemed a waste, if you ask me. You'd make a fine Archangel, Xai. Join us and I'll guarantee you a kingdom on Earth."

I scratched my jaw as if considering his insane offer. On a practical level, I understood his proposal. With my experience, age, and strength, maintaining a territory would be within my realm of ability and birthright. "I've never much cared for humans," I mused out loud. Not a lie, but a fact. The only reason I ever tolerated humanity was for Evangeline.

She glanced at me sharply. "Don't you dare."

"It's a reasonable proposal," I pointed out emotionlessly.

Her gaze narrowed, disapproval radiating off her. "You can't be serious."

I wasn't, and if she didn't know that by now, we had a serious problem. Trusting she understood my motives better than she portrayed, I ignored her and met Dariel's gaze. "My father put me on Earth because he knew I was stronger than him." Not a lie, I just didn't elaborate on why. "It's not my favorite plane by any means, but owning a small territory may make it more pleasant." I tapped my chin and shrugged. "Say I'm interested. What would you need from me in return?"

Evangeline grabbed my arm, her nails digging into my flesh. "You can't fucking be serious."

I gave her a patient look. "Quiet, darling, the Archangels are talking."

She growled while Dariel chuckled. "Yes, Evangeline, quiet."

It took all manner of restraint not to punch the imbecile for talking to Evangeline in that manner. I hadn't actually meant my words. But he did.

I cocked an impatient brow. "What would you need from me, Dariel?" I repeated.

"Help destroying the portals, for one."

"You can't manage that task on your own?" I asked, feigning surprise. "I assumed you were the one creating the gateways between Hell and Heaven." A false statement meant to entice the truth. *Who is helping you, Dariel?* I wondered.

"That's a group effort," he replied vaguely. "But you and I both know the ritual requires beings on both sides."

I nodded, understanding. "You need me to take a side and assist with the ancient chants." Which stirred another fascinating question. "Who originally agreed to help with the task?"

"Me," a feminine voice replied from above.

"You're joking," Evangeline breathed, her lips parting in shock as Lucía descended the stairs. "Your purpose in life is to uphold the balance."

"Is it?" she asked, stopping at Dariel's side to lay her dark head against his shoulder. "I'm a piece of the Divinity stationed in the underworld. How is that balanced?"

"You're going to destroy everything we've worked so

hard to create," Evangeline argued, her love for humanity taking over. "How many innocent lives will be lost?"

"How do you survive this?" Dariel asked me, waving a hand over Evangeline.

By loving her. "It's not without effort," I replied flatly. "But that belies the point of our meeting, and as we're surrounded, I suggest we focus on what matters. Why do you need me to help with the portal when you have Lucía?"

"While I've taught her the chants, she's not as powerful as the son of two Archangels."

"Meaning you already tried and failed," I translated, the foreign part of me shining more insight into the situation. "So you orchestrated this scene and had Lucía send a warning that you knew my mother would foresee."

Excitement danced in his multicolored eyes, giving him a maniacal glow that confirmed his lack of sanity. "I knew you were the right candidate for this, Xai."

It disturbed me that he felt so confident in that assumption. What vibe had I given off that would ever convince someone I'd be inclined to destroy Heaven?

Still, it lent me an advantage. I needed Dariel away from all these lives, and he'd provided me with the perfect opportunity.

"I accept." The words came easily, as did the shrug of my shoulders that followed.

Evangeline gasped beside me, her blue eyes swirling with fury as she glowered up at me. I held her gaze with disinterest. "Come now, love, surely you see this is the best way?"

"You know I don't." The hurt in her expression had me second-guessing this game. Did she truly believe me capable of such horror? No. No, she *knew* me. Our souls were bound together for eternity. She had to see through this, had to understand...

A sharp pang to my chest settled my resolve.

Heaven is Falling.

I could *feel* it.

"Do come back soon. We need you."

My mother's prophetic words validated my decision. "Lucía, would you mind keeping Evangeline company while Dariel and I see this through?"

The lethal assassin beside me twirled her blades, her stance ready for a fight. "Good luck with that."

I sighed, truly irritated by the notion of her not having any faith in me at all. After everything we'd been through, she had to see through it.

Please don't break my heart now...

"Evangeline—" I caught her knife with one hand—by the sharp end—and her wrist with my other hand. Then I spun her into the wall, dropped her blade, and covered her mouth with my bloody palm when she started to growl. My thighs pinned hers against the wall while my forearm dug into her throat. "Be a good girl and keep Lucía company while I work with Dariel. We can continue this conversation after the portals are destroyed."

Defiance and hatred radiated from her, causing my soul to wither inside me.

She didn't trust me.

How many times would I have to explain—

Evangeline's tongue lightly traced the wound her blade had made against my palm and swallowed. Deliberately.

Her eyes sang a song of loathing, putting on a show for everyone around us, but inside, my mate was ready.

"I can see that you're not going to play nice while I'm

gone," I said, sounding disappointed. "You've really left me with no choice, love."

My forearm tensed against her throat, suffocating her.

She made to fight me, her nails clawing at my skin while she continued to lick my palm in reassurance.

It physically hurt to do this to her, especially as her eyes glazed with angry tears. "You'll forgive me later," I whispered, removing my palm to kiss her just before her legs gave out. I loosened my grip just enough to allow her a semblance of breath and exhaled softly into her mouth. Then I let her fall to the ground in a heap of violet feathers —my favorite color.

"I suggest you tie her up," I said to Lucía. "And we should go. Alastor isn't going to make this easy."

"Actually, he's already been handled," Dariel replied with an affectionate look at Lucía. "She's truly brilliant."

I pretended to be impressed. "You'll have to explain that."

"Another time." He gestured to the still-open door. "Lead the way, Son of Chaos."

"Happily," I replied, meaning it.

I stepped through the threshold and took to the sky with a sharp burst from my wings. Most required a running start or starting on a higher ledge, but even after millennia without my feathers, I could take off from a standstill.

A measure of strength and fortitude, my father would always say.

Dariel lifted with the same ease, his coloring immediately shifting to match his surroundings—a chameleon by nature. I studied his energy patterns and measured his movements, preparing for the inevitable. Portals were always situated outside of populated areas, as that allowed for better regulation and control. I just needed to guide him close enough to push.

I subtly stretched my muscles as we flew, my mind shifting through various strategies and methods.

I'd never fought an Archangel. Not truly. It would require tapping into my deepest resources, finding everything my birthright had ever gifted me, and using it against him.

To destroy Dariel, I needed to diminish his light and deplete his energy reserves. An idea surfaced in my mind, morphing into a plan with multiple paths and avenues, all yielding similar outcomes.

Destiny...

I listened while I flew, taking in every detail and move, seeing every potential result.

Yes.

This could work.

I just had to play it right.

The portal shone in the distance, its magnetic fields drawing me to its power source. As my chosen path unfolded before me, I closed my eyes and stole a deep breath.

Now.

CHAPTER 17

I Have No Idea What Side I'm On Anymore

Five Minutes Earlier...

Be safe, my soul whispered.

Xai didn't reply. Not that I expected him to.

The door closed behind him with a finality that sent a bolt of fear through my heart.

The second Xai had agreed to hear out Dariel's insanity plea—because, really, that's what it was—I knew his intention.

He intended to fight, and to do that, he needed Dariel as far away from the city as he could manage. Because Archangels were destructive.

And as much as I wanted to join Xai in taking that crazy bastard down, I knew I would only distract him. His bloodline painted this as his duty, while mine granted me a different task.

Lucía.

Why were all the ancient beings insane? Yes, living for eternity caused boredom, but how would a war solve that? If they wanted to die, all they needed to do was ask.

Daughter of Death reporting for duty.
First up? Lucía.
Weapon of choice? Throwing blade.
Location? Preferably—

"Before you go into surprise attack mode—which won't be a surprise because I already know your plan—please hear me out." Lucía's words cut into my mental play-by-play, causing me to frown. "Just... you can sit up now, and hold a knife if it makes you feel better, but I beg you to let me explain."

I hadn't heard anyone else enter the house, so she was clearly speaking to me. Yet, her words made no sense.

"I'm not really working with Dariel," she continued. "And I can prove it if you give me five minutes."

Okay, she had my attention now. I lifted my head and met her patient gaze. Typically, this was the moment where I sought out the blackness in her essence, but it didn't rise, didn't even flinch.

Justice not required, my lethal soul whispered.

Well, that was new. I narrowed my gaze at her. She claimed that she could prove her innocence. "Prove it how?" I demanded.

"Alastor."

My eyebrows shot upward. "The Archdemon you supposedly took care of?"

She licked her lips and nodded. "Dariel thinks I poisoned him with silver. Alastor made a show of collapsing from the clouds right after you walked in the door, which is how I kept Dariel from leaving. After seeing Alastor fall, he felt more confident in his ability to take on Xai, had he refused the offer." She ran her fingers through her long strands, her shoulders hunching. "I've been playing on his side for over a hundred years and reporting everything to Alastor. He'll confirm it. I promise."

Her promise didn't mean much to me, especially after—

The hairs along my arm danced as electricity hummed through the air.

It's starting...

I jumped to my feet, my heart racing.

Xai.

An explosion sounded in the distance.

"He didn't waste time," Lucía said, her lips curling warily. "I hope he destroys Dariel."

I ignored her, my soul searching for its other half and finding him thriving.

He's okay.

Tremors shook the ground, the building around us groaning from the unexpected impact.

Two Archangels.

Fighting in Hell.

The balance of our worlds is shattering.

My stomach twisted. *How has it come to this?*

Another crash ended in demonic screams and screeches, sending a chill down my spine.

But Xai's lifeline beat steadily with mine.

Still alive.

The door flew open, Alastor filling the entry with his dark wings, his gaze wild and searching for Lucía. She ran into his open arms, her face against his neck as he held her with a tenderness that shocked me.

That surprise was short-lived as Trudy entered behind them, her expression annoyed. "Someone needs to get up there and help him."

"Agreed," Alastor replied, his lips against Lucía's forehead. "You're all right?"

She nodded, her throat working. "Ending him is only the beginning."

"I know, sweetheart." He kissed her temple, holding her close. "But we have to start somewhere." His chocolate eyes lifted to mine. "Stay here."

I scowled at him. "I don't report to you."

Arrogance and superiority straightened his spine, his broad shoulders appearing wider and more intimidating in his elegant suit. "You need to protect everyone on the ground, and Xai can't focus if you're up there. If—"

"I know," I snapped, annoyed that he was wasting precious time. "Stop stating the obvious and get up there and help him take that asshole down."

Respect reflected in his gaze as he gave me a nod. "If anything happens to Lucía, I'll kill you." He stepped backward and took flight without so much as a jump.

I snorted. "Keep dreaming, Archdemon."

"Since when are you and Alastor an item?" Trudy demanded.

Lucía actually blushed, her lips curling. "It's new, but—"

"Seriously? That's what you two want to talk about right now?" I shook my head and collected my knives.

First things first, the body in the living room.

I swiped Trudy's sword from her waist before she could react and walked around the coffee table to Grant's unconscious form. "May you rest in Hell," I growled, swiping the sword through the air and severing his head.

Fast.

Quick.

And far too painless.

His black soul, almost slimy in texture, slithered into

the air and slowly joined all the others I carried with me—the burden of Death.

I swallowed, my eyes closing just for a moment as I soothed the darkness, morphing it into light, and welcomed him for eternity.

Justice served.

Yes.

Trudy and Lucía were both watching me warily when I finally opened my eyes again. "What?"

"Nothing, you just..." Trudy trailed off.

"Went all eerily quiet and smiled," Lucía finished. "Like you enjoyed killing him."

"I'm the Daughter of Death." I wiped the sword against Grant's leg before twirling it in my palm and handing it to Trudy, handle first. "You're going to need that."

Her brow crinkled. "I am?"

"You are."

"Why?" she asked.

"Because we're going to Heaven to kill some intruders." I didn't wait for them to reply, just walked out the door and into the stifling air. We needed to find one of those portals, or a being strong enough to take us upward.

Lightning crashed in the sky, sending a jolt through my heart.

A glance up showed Xai tumbling backward, his black wings spiraling around him as he started to fall.

I froze, my lips parted on a silent scream.

Don't you dare! You get back up and fight him!

Another bolt flew through the air from an undetectable source, nailing Xai's wings. Flames erupted around him, his feathers burning before my eyes.

I started running without thinking, my wings flaring and taking me to the sky.

A flash of black light exploded from Xai, my heart breaking at the sight.

No!

I flew faster, my shoulders protesting. I needed to catch him, to save him...

Another blast rocked the clouds, the sky dimming beneath the midnight shades.

What is that? The sky fracturing?

Darkness shrouded the lands, covered the sun, swallowing us all into an inky abyss.

I paused midflight, the opaque surroundings making it impossible to see.

I can't catch you... My ribs cracked beneath the pressure, a sob ripping its way from my throat. *Xai!*

I'm all right, love, he whispered.

Thunder rumbled through the clouds, followed by a burst of heat and sound. The wind sent me downward, forcing me to land while sand and debris kicked up around me.

I can't see anything.

I know, he replied. *And neither can Dariel.*

Another clap of thunder shook the ground, sending me to my ass. Lightning zipped above, the only light for miles, and then a deafening crack sounded.

The sun broke through the ink-stained sky, radiating warmth and highlighting a gorgeous blue sky devoid of angels.

I blinked. *Xai?*

No reply.

I forced myself to my feet and spun in a circle, searching.

Nothing.

With a running start, I jumped and soared high.

Several buildings were destroyed from lightning strikes, and the erratic weather had stirred up sand all throughout the city, but Xai and Dariel were nowhere to be seen.

The portal in the distance still thrived.

Nothing else had severely changed.

Where are you? I demanded.

If he heard me, he didn't reply.

I hurried back to where I left Trudy and Lucía, and found them waiting for me with a windblown Alastor. "Where did they go?"

He shook his head. "I don't know."

"What do you mean, you don't know?"

He didn't repeat himself, just shook his head again.

I opened my mouth to demand he try harder, but my voice failed me as pain unlike anything I'd ever felt ripped me apart from the inside. My knees gave out beneath me, sending me crashing to the ground on a soundless scream.

Xai.

His spirit.

I felt it ripping me in half, tearing away from my being, my essence, my *soul*.

Tears froze in my eyes, too shocked to fall.

Our bond...was...shattering.

My name fell from those around me, panic filling their voices.

Xai...

He couldn't do this to me.

No.

No.

No!

I curled into a ball, my insides rioting, my heart disintegrating.

Broken irrevocably.

Destroyed.

Half of me had just...died.

The better half.

The only half that had ever mattered.

My Xai...

I trusted you to come back to me.

I trusted you to never leave me.

You promised to follow me.

You can't leave me now.

How could you do this to me?

How could you?

My other half. My mate. My only love.

I'll hate you forever for this.

And never stop loving you.

Don't do this to me!

Don't you dare do this to me!

But it was too late.

It didn't matter what I said.

Because he was already gone.

"I can't feel him..." I whispered to no one but myself. "He's... he's gone."

CHAPTER 18
SHADOW DEMONS SUCK. LITERALLY

Several Minutes Earlier...

I tucked and rolled through the humid air, my feathers sizzling from the lightning bolt Dariel had thrown at me.

The bastard had good fucking aim.

I needed a new plan. Alastor's affinity for disease was useless against an Archangel, thereby rendering him to the strength of a warrior alone.

No. I required something catastrophic.

Another jolt hit my side, this one hotter and inciting flames all around me. Everything burned—my wings, my skin, my very being destroyed beneath the fiery embers.

He's going to win, I realized. Dariel was stronger, faster, an ancient like my parents, and he'd somehow tapped into this plane's energy fields. He should be suffering as a being of Heaven, but the Archangel of Concealment was definitely thriving.

No! Evangeline's shout pierced my thoughts, her concern palpable.

She's watching me fail. I frowned at the thought. She'd trusted me to handle this, had expected me to finish it. Because I *should* be able to.

Yes, Dariel had found a way to prosper down here, but chaos *reigned* in Hell.

I closed my eyes and turned inward, ignoring the pain, my free fall, and everything else around me.

Show me, I demanded. *Show me what I'm missing.*

The Archangel within me—the one I kept on a tight leash—flourished in my mind, blossoming into a sea of darkness that urged me to play.

Chaos.

Destiny.

Intertwined.

I smiled. *Yes.*

That foreign part of me bloomed, revealing a path I understood. The future, the past, the present, all intertwined into a fate I had no choice but to accept.

My eyes flew open.

The world had gone as dark as my mind, but I could see. My wings no longer burned, my being already healed.

It's time.

I know.

Dariel drew himself in circles above, his panic a beautiful sight. He'd considered me defeated, the baby Archangel who had never truly realized his purpose.

Until now.

I can't catch you... Evangeline's choked thoughts gave me pause, her terror desperate for a reply. *Xai!*

I'm all right, love, I whispered, sending her calming vibes as I silently floated upward toward my target in the clouds.

There was only one place I could take Dariel where he

would surely die. But I had to get close enough to catch him off guard.

I crept higher, his anxiety coming off him in sparks as he tried futilely to blend into the black smog. My lips curled in anticipation.

Just a few feet away...

He whirled, sensing me, and created a wave of spinning power that spun through the air, creating thunder in the sky around us.

But he'd sent it the wrong way.

I can't see anything. Evangeline sounded so frustrated.

I know, I replied. *And neither can Dariel.*

I wrapped my arm around his neck and yanked. His spine severed with a snap, rendering him temporarily paralyzed but very aware. "Hello, Dariel," I murmured, my teleportation gift already engaged.

A map of the underworld revealed itself before my eyes, responding to my darkness and allowing me free roam.

"I have a treat for you," I told him softly as I navigated us toward the last place I ever wanted to visit again. "You're going to hate it."

Evangeline's panic speared my heart, causing me to hesitate only briefly.

No, I would be all right. She had to know that. But I couldn't risk her being with me here. Not after what happened last time.

My soul withered and cried out while my mind locked on our precious link and forcibly blocked her lifeline. It was the best way to protect her. She would understand. I hoped.

An ache immediately formed in my heart at her loss, my angelic spirit mourning her as if she'd died. Tears graced my eyes, my insides empty without her presence, and I embraced it. Required it. Fed from it.

I'm vacant.

The Shadow realm unveiled before me, the wispy veils of smoke already rushing to greet their new meal. Except it wasn't me they wanted to feast upon, but the stirring Archangel in my arms.

He'd been conscious the whole time, his eyes wild with confusion.

"You thought I intended to take you home for justice," I murmured with a smile. "Oh, no. That's not how I operate." I dropped him in the fields.

His lips parted on a scream that didn't grace the air.

His body convulsed as the beings of this plane leapt on him with an eagerness that would have terrified some of the harshest creatures of the underworld.

One of the shadowed figures glanced at me in interest, and I cocked a brow. "Try it."

The demon actually recoiled.

I smirked. "I didn't think so." Whatever I'd done in Alastor's realm had clearly carried with me, granting me dominion over this horrid plane. But it certainly served a reasonable purpose.

Dariel stood no chance, his light withering by the second. How Evangeline had survived more than a few minutes here remained a mystery. It was a testament to her vigor and resilience.

My stomach churned at the thought of her, how she must feel, but I had no choice. I would bring no piece of her here. She'd suffered enough. It was my turn now.

"Any final words?" I asked Dariel, noting his inability to speak. "Hmm, no, I suppose not."

His cheekbones protruded through his skin as the Shadow demons sucked the remains of his life through his skin. A ghastly sight that I refused to look away from. He began to shrivel, the last vestiges of his soul disappearing into the gray abyss.

"As Evangeline would say, 'May you rest in Hell.'" I grinned with the words, finding them incredibly appropriate as the Archangel disintegrated into ash. The Shadow demons grumbled in disappointment. "Good to know you can be helpful," I murmured. "But if you ever touch my Evangeline again, I will come back here and destroy every last one of you."

A few of them took a step back, clearly receiving my message.

"Excellent." I stood and stretched my aching sides. "Until next time."

I focused my energy on finding Alastor's realm again, needing my Evangeline. It'd only been a few minutes, but it felt like an eternity without her.

Our bond flickered.

Sizzled.

Died.

My brow furrowed. That was not supposed to happen. Though, I supposed, neither was cutting her off.

I tried again, her lifeline barely a whisper in my mind.

Such pain...

It seared my insides, scorching my soul.

Evangeline!

Something had happened. Something catastrophic. I could feel her shattered being just out of my reach, refusing my call.

Where are you? I demanded. The easy connection we had before no longer existed, her essence a haunted chasm refusing me entry.

I burst into Alastor's realm from the sky, my gaze already searching. The place I'd felt her last was vacant.

Had she flown back to the others? Had someone taken her again?

Fire licked through my veins at the thought. I would burn this world down trying to find her.

And here I'd promised never to leave her side.

She could defend herself, I knew that, trusted in that, but what if she'd been caught unawares again?

"Evangeline!" I yelled, my voice carrying over the wind and bellowing through the realm. Everything and everyone seemed to still beneath me. It took me a moment to realize why—I'd begun blackening the sky again.

That unique trait was both a blessing and a curse.

Alastor appeared in the sky, his brown feathers carrying a reddish tint from the sun. He started toward me, and I met him halfway. "Where is she?"

"On the ground," he replied as if that explained everything. "How the fuck did you do that?"

"Where, Alastor?" I didn't want to play the question game. I wanted my mate.

He sighed dramatically. "No one employs common conversational skills anymore. It's all work and no fun." He turned, his path leading us toward his palatial estate. "I assume Dariel is dead?"

"Very," I replied, at least giving him that.

"Good. Of course, now we don't know whom he was working with."

"Time will inform us," the dark part of me murmured.

"How cryptic," he deadpanned as he took a sharp turn.

Evangeline's purple feathers were scattered across the ground, her body crumpled into a ball between Lucía and Trudy. I dropped behind them, my fury palpable. "Do not touch her."

Both women jumped back, their expressions shocked. I

eyed Lucía with disgust and raised a brow when Alastor landed in front of her. "Touch her, and we'll have a problem, Archangel."

I didn't care enough to ask. If Evangeline had let the woman live, there had to be a good reason.

She didn't move or acknowledge me, her feathers wilting before my eyes.

"What happened?" I growled, needing to know whom to kill.

"You, uh, died," Trudy replied slowly.

"Do I look dead to you?" I asked her, my brow arching.

"No, but she thought..." She trailed off, or perhaps continued; I wasn't sure because I stopped listening.

Evangeline thought I was dead.

My heart skipped a beat, my soul still aching for its mate to acknowledge him.

Oh, darling...

I knelt beside her, pulling her into my arms. She remained still, her face ashen, her body weak.

Breaking from her, even briefly, had zapped the strength of will right out of her. My strong, fierce assassin was broken because of me.

I touched my forehead to hers. "I'm so sorry, love. I couldn't take any part of you with me. Not after what happened."

If she heard me, she didn't acknowledge it.

I sighed, looking up at Alastor. "Do you require us for anything else?"

His dark brows rose. "You ventured into my realm, Archangel. Not by my invitation, I might add. So are *you* finished fighting Archangels in my realm?"

I considered all the avenues of his question, all the possibilities I knew would come to be, and sighed. "Likely not, but I am today." There were still others to hunt down —nameless and faceless individuals who needed to pay for the imbalance. Dariel had implied they were in Heaven already, wreaking havoc as we worked, but I knew that to be a lie. Yes, something had shifted, but my realm was still safe. Nothing and no one had Fallen.

"You'll see us again, and soon," I told him. "A new power arises in your realm, Alastor. I wish you luck, as you'll need it." The words came unbidden and I wasn't quite sure what they implied, but I had to say them.

I'm becoming my mother, I growled.

And from the look on Alastor's face, he was not pleased by it. "Take your prophecies back to Heaven, Archangel. I prefer to live in the moment."

I smirked. "Likewise." I held Evangeline close and nodded a goodbye before triggering our ascent.

CHAPTER 19

XAI'S RELATIONSHIP ADVICE 101: FORGIVENESS IS IMPORTANT

Night had fallen over Heaven by the time we returned, the moon shining beautifully over our favorite field.

As I sensed, the walls were fine. Something had shifted earlier, causing the sensations we experienced in Hell, but I didn't care about that now. The woman in my arms had my complete and undivided attention.

"Evangeline," I whispered, laying her on the ground beneath me. Her wings had melted to ash and rebloomed upon our entry, her luscious purple plumes glistening in the moonlight. "Open your eyes."

She shook her head, as stubborn as ever.

I brushed my lips across her jaw, her neck, along her collarbone. "Please," I whispered. "I need to see your eyes, love."

She whimpered in reply, a fractured sound I never wanted to hear from her again.

"You still think me dead." We played this game once before, what felt like decades ago in Earth years. "Open your eyes," I repeated more forcefully.

Her lashes fluttered, her lips trembling.

"I promise you'll like what you see." I added a hint of underlining arrogance in hopes of coaxing her, but that only seemed to increase her quivering. "Where's my warrior? Why are you hiding?"

"You died." Two broken words that hurt to hear.

I remained on my knees, straddling her hips, and cupped her face between my palms. "No, I temporarily cut off our link to guard you from the Shadow realm."

Her brow furrowed, understanding finally carving a path into her beautiful features. "You what?"

"I'm not repeating myself." She heard me the first time.

Sapphire irises appeared, fire simmering in their depth. "You *what*?"

Oh, this I preferred to the sadness.

Fire.

Fury.

A fight.

"Why would you do that?" she asked, her voice strengthening. "You cut me off?"

"To protect you, love." I drew my thumb across her reddening cheek. "After what they did to you last time, I wanted no possibility of them touching you again."

"So you severed our link?" She shoved against my shoulders with far more power than I anticipated, knocking me to the side. I caught her hips, pulling her over me before she could escape, causing her breasts to touch my chest again.

"Yes," I replied softly. "I wanted to keep you safe."

"I thought you died!" she snapped, her palm nearly cracking my face. I grasped her wrists and rolled her beneath me once more.

Stretching her arms out over her head with one hand, I

used my other to circle her throat. "I'm here, Evangeline, and very much alive."

"And very much an asshole."

I shrugged. "A fact that will never change."

"I thought you died, Xai," she repeated, her eyes misting. "Do you have any idea what that felt like?"

"Yes," I whispered, my grip loosening on her hands. "I felt empty inside without you, and still do since you haven't allowed me to reinstate the bond."

She said nothing for a moment, her lashes falling. "Maybe you don't deserve it anymore." The words were so quiet I almost didn't hear them.

"You can't mean that," I said, sitting up with my legs straddled across her thighs. "Take that back."

She didn't meet my gaze. Didn't speak.

"Evangeline," I whispered, my heart breaking all over again. "Tell me you didn't mean that."

"You cut me off," she replied softly, her lower lip trembling. "*You,* Xai. Not me."

"To protect you," I repeated yet again. "What would you have me do, Evangeline? Keep the connection alive in a realm that nearly stole you from me?"

Her blue eyes finally grasped mine and held fiercely. "I survived in that realm because of my link to you. Because of my will to return to you, Xai. Don't you see?" Sadness radiated from her gaze, destroying me from the inside out.

"Removing that bond, blocking it in any way, weakens us both," she continued, her voice soft. "You turned me away in a moment where I needed to know you were alive, in a moment where I was so terrified I may never see you again after seeing you on fire, and I thought you were gone forever. *That* damaged me more than the Shadow realm ever could, Xai."

Agony radiated from her, serving as a hint of what I'd done by closing her off. "I never meant to hurt you."

"But you did," she whispered. "More than I ever thought possible." The resolve in her expression nearly destroyed me.

She couldn't... Not now. Not ever.

I dropped my head to her chest, my body shaking above hers. "Don't do this, Evangeline. Please, don't do this." I grasped her shoulders, holding her as if I could keep her here for eternity. "I thought I was protecting you, I thought... I couldn't bear the thought of the Shadows touching you again. Not after almost losing you, after finding you on the edge of death. You have to see that, have to understand it."

"And you need to see why breaking our bond wasn't the answer. You harmed us more by pushing me away, Xai. You can't do that. You can't ever do that to me again." She grabbed my hair, forcing me upward. "Do you hear me? Trust me to defend myself. Trust yourself to defend me too. But don't ever shut me out. I'd prefer death to the feeling of losing you."

Tears rolled down her cheeks at the words, matching the streaks lancing my heart. "I acted on instinct. Protecting you will always be my primary objective."

She sighed. "You have no idea how much it hurt to feel you disappear."

"But I do, love. I felt it when you were in the Shadow realms." I held her gaze, begging her to understand. "I couldn't experience that again."

"Yet you did by closing me off."

"Yes, but I knew you were okay."

"But I didn't!" she cried out. "I didn't know you were okay, Xai. I thought you were gone. Forever. Always.

Leaving me behind to live a solitary existence, never to be the same. Alone. Dead. I would have preferred death to that fate."

Fuck. After everything we'd been through, *this* was what finally drew a line for her. Part of me understood. I'd messed up by not communicating again, not warning her before I severed the link. The other part of me had no regrets. I would never allow those dark beings anywhere near her again.

"I'm sorry, Evangeline," I whispered. "I'm sorry for scaring you. But I'm here. I'll always be here. Don't walk away from us now, not after everything, not over this." I begged her with my lips, tasting her skin, memorizing every inch of her face. "Don't push me away, please. You're scared and angry, and I understand, but don't end this."

She quivered beneath me, tears rolling down her cheeks. "I hate you," she said, and I knew she meant it. "I love you. I fucking hate how much I love you." Her hand fisted in my hair as she pulled. "It hurts, Xai. Everything hurts."

"Because you're fighting the truth of us," I told her. "You're depriving our souls of their rightful bond."

"Because you broke it."

"I did," I admitted. "For a reason I've explained. You're the one hurting us now."

She shuddered, her eyes closing. "I'm afraid."

"That I'll sever the ties again," I said, finishing her statement.

"Yes. No." She shook her head. "I'm afraid that if I let you in, I'll find out none of this is real and it's just my mind playing tricks on me again. That you really died and that if I open again, you won't really be there."

"I'm right here, Evangeline."

"I know, and I know it's ridiculous, but you *died*, Xai."

"I didn't. I'm here."

She whimpered, her head swaying back and forth. "My heart can't handle this."

"Neither can mine, love. Let me back in, let me love you, let me fix this."

"You can't."

"I can." I took her mouth in a kiss filled with all our thousands of years together. The memories, the fights, the love, the hot, unbridled passion. I unleashed it all, forcing her to let me in, demanding she trust me again, to see why I blocked her, to understand my deep, undying devotion to her.

She was my life. My reason. My mate.

"I love you," I whispered. "I'm sorry I hurt you. I can't promise not to do it again, because we both know that's impossible. You're killing me now, and may again in the future, but I wouldn't hold it against you, love. I'll fight for you. I'll fight for us. And I need you to fight for us too."

Her breaths were harsh against my lips, her cheeks damp from crying, her body quivering beneath mine. I kissed her again, less harshly, more lovingly, and waited for her to reciprocate, a part of me dying with each passing second.

"You're punishing me," I whispered, pained at her lack of a response. "I'm sorry, Evangeline. I said I was sorry. Please don't send me away. I need you. I always have, always will. I—"

Her mouth captured mine, silencing my plea, and I sagged against her, destroyed. Losing her would be my end. She had to see that, had to know that.

Her tongue slipped into my mouth, fueling my need to possess her, to reclaim my mate. "Evangeline," I breathed.

She kissed me again, more demanding this time, her nails trailing down my arms to my stomach, to my waist. Her fingers moved over my belt, unfastening as she went, her intentions clear. I let her lead us, own us, remake us.

My palms cradled her face, holding on for dear life, *needing* her. "Evangeline," I repeated, my breath leaving on a hiss as she pulled my cock free. "I love you."

She didn't return the endearment, her mouth silencing mine again as she unfastened her own clothes, kicking off her pants and mine, and wrapping her legs around my waist. "Fuck me," she demanded. "Hard, Xai. I need it hard."

I pressed my forehead to hers, sliding inside her waiting heat. "If this is you trying to say goodbye, I won't let you," I told her, thrusting sharply. "You can't punish me forever, Evangeline. Not for doing something we both know was justified."

Her nails scored my sides, her hips bucking to meet mine. "You *died*, Xai."

"I'm here, Evangeline," I growled, shoving home to prove it. "Let me back in and I'll prove it."

She shuddered, her lips parting on a groan. I felt her resistance melting, her body welcoming me home, her soul rejoicing at being so near.

"You love me," I whispered.

"I do," she agreed. "But I hate you, too."

"I know." I increased my pace, fucking her into the oblivion I knew she adored. "That part will never change." It was part of what made us click, that fiery passion, the anger, the fury, the tension, the explosive chemistry, and the dark understanding between our souls.

She groaned as I shifted my hips in a way I knew she enjoyed, her thighs tensing around me. "I can't resist you," she whispered, her eyes closing in ecstasy. "Have never been able to."

"Because you don't want to," I told her, dropping my lips to her neck to nip her pulse. *Let me rekindle our bond, love*, my soul whispered, my teeth skimming her tender skin.

"Yes," she hissed, whether in agreement to my vocalized statement or to the unspoken request I'd made against her neck, I didn't know.

So I kissed her instead, trailing a path up to her ear. "Let me back in, love. Complete us again."

I struck her deep, eliciting a beautiful sound from her throat in the process. Not agreement, but definitely approval of my actions.

"You can use me all you want, Evangeline, but we both know who will win this game." I slowed my movements in demonstration, my pelvis just barely rubbing her clit. "Give in before I make you beg, love."

She shuddered beneath me. "Xai..."

"Evangeline," I returned, my voice a deep growl. "Stop making me wait or I'll return the favor."

"I've not forgiven you yet."

"But you will."

She sighed, lacing her fingers through my hair as she tugged to bring my face away from her neck. Her blue eyes shone brightly in the moonlight, her gaze holding mine. "I will," she agreed softly. "But if you ever do that to me again, I'll kill you myself."

My lips curled. "That almost sounds like foreplay, darling."

"I mean it, Xai. If you do that to me again, I *will* kill you."

"Now you're just turning me on," I teased.

She thrust upward. "Already there, jackass. Now take me seriously."

"I always take you seriously."

"Liar," she accused, scowling.

"Never," I whispered, taking her mouth in a kiss meant to smooth out her frown. My cock slid deep inside her, then out, and slowly in again. Not our usual dance, but it felt right to cherish her. "If there is ever a need for me to do it again, I will warn you first," I promised her. I couldn't promise not to do it again, because I refused to endanger her in any way, and she had to understand that.

She bit my lower lip in retribution, hard enough to bleed, then laved the wound with her tongue. I shuddered at the contact and what it implied. *Acceptance.*

I nipped her in return, drawing blood and pulling the essence into my mouth.

One swallow initiated the bond.

Another lick solidified it.

My heart skipped a beat, my soul rejoicing at the rekindled connection, my being complete once again. Evangeline's quiver said she felt it too, and her kiss told me she approved.

I returned her embrace, took control of it, and powered us through it.

Mine.

My spirit required I reclaim her fully, and from the way she met me move for move, I knew her soul agreed.

"Xai," she panted, my name never sounding sweeter. "Now."

I chuckled, my lips at her neck again. "Always so impatient," I murmured, my hand sliding between us to find that sweet spot she craved. My thumb drifted over her teasingly, and she arched into me on a groan that went straight to my balls. "I love that sound."

She did it again, this time highlighting it with a curse coupled with my name.

"More," I demanded, needing her to lose herself to our passion.

I unleashed my strength, my body dominating hers in the way we both adored. She took what I gave her and returned it full throttle, our bodies the perfect match for one another in every way.

Another downward stroke had her walls clamping around me, her body freezing in the initial throes of a climax that ripped a scream from her throat. I pumped into her hard, chasing after her orgasm with one of my own, my muscles strained from the effort, my heart thudding in ecstasy.

"Mine," she growled, causing my lips to curl. That was usually my line.

"Yours," I agreed, my lips against hers. "For eternity."

CHAPTER 20

HOW MANY DEATHS DOES IT TAKE TO EARN A VACATION?

I couldn't find my clothes, but at least I had my wings. My feathers nudged Xai's as we flew to his home in the heart of the city.

He chuckled. "I thought you were still mad at me."

"I am."

"Then why are you flirting, love?"

"Because I also want to fuck you again," I replied honestly.

His dark gaze caught mine, a glimmer in their depths. "My insatiable Evangeline."

"Yes, it's such a hardship for you," I deadpanned.

"Truly difficult," he agreed, smirking. "But I suspect we'll have company when we return."

I frowned. "Who?"

"My mother," he murmured. "I'm not sure how I know that, but I do."

I considered that as we flew, my thoughts returning to Alastor's realm. "You blackened the sky."

"I did." He twirled in the sky, his midnight plumes dancing with his movements. "You inspired me, Evangeline. I realized I was failing you, and I couldn't allow that." He glanced back, his dark hair blowing in the wind stirred by his flight. "Does my new ability scare you?"

"No." The only thing that ever frightened me was the thought of losing him. "Does it scare you?"

"I've always favored the dark, so no," he murmured. "It felt... right."

We landed on his balcony, our hands finding each other immediately as he pulled me into him, his larger wings circling around us and covering mine in an angelic hug. I thought he meant to kiss me until he said, "Hello, Mother."

"Xai," she returned from just inside. "You're late."

"Evangeline distracted me."

I pinched his side, which caused him to chuckle and his mother to tsk. "Blaming your mate for your own antics. What kind of son have I raised?"

A cryptic one, I thought with a snort.

Xai's gaze narrowed, his hands moved to my hips to pull me closer. "I heard that."

I raised a brow. *You did?*

"I did," he replied, nuzzling my nose. *Seems our bond has strengthened,* he added mentally. *I approve.* "How can I be late, Mother, when we both know you knew when to anticipate my arrival?"

I couldn't see her, but I heard her chuckle. "Touché." A soft ruffle of feathers followed, indicating her movement. "I came to talk to you about the imbalance, as I'm sure you felt it."

"Dariel claimed it to be the portals reopening."

She snorted. "That jackass knows nothing. I've been watching his choices for centuries, as well as all the others—"

"You know who else is involved?" Xai asked, interrupting her.

"Of course. I see all their fates, child, and soon, you will too. Or glimpses, anyway. Dariel's demise is just the beginning. Others will lay claim to his former role and pick up the broken pieces. That's why I'm here."

"To talk about our future. Not to give us their identities so we can stop them preemptively." Xai phrased it as a statement, not a question.

"Destiny will happen with or without my involvement, something you'll one day understand. If I alter the path of one, it alters the paths of others, but the end results still happen. So I allow it to play out while positioning my pawns accordingly."

"Such as sending us to Hell," I said, unsure of how I felt about being referred to as a "pawn."

"Precisely, and you both influenced the others appropriately. Now, we wait, and learn, and grow. Which brings me back to the imbalance. Surely by now you've felt the changes, yes?"

"Sort of hard to miss the midnight sky," I replied while holding Xai's gaze. He smirked in response but remained silent otherwise.

"Everything is shifting, not just in Hell but in Heaven too. Have you ever wondered why you were placed on Earth?" she asked.

"I've always assumed you had a purpose," Xai replied. "Aside from destroying my relationship with Evangeline, I imagine you wished to teach me about humanity."

"Your relationship together is strong because of everything you've endured." The affection in her voice made it hard to dislike her for playing a game of chess with our lives. Hard, but not impossible. "And yes, humanity, Xai.

You required the experience more than anyone else because of who you have now become."

He finally looked away from me, his gaze traveling over my shoulder to the female behind me. "And who is that?"

"Don't you see? Chaos favors the night, while destiny thrives in the light, but you embody the gray. Both entities in one, my child."

Xai blinked. "You're speaking to me in riddles."

She stomped her foot. "I am not. This makes perfect sense. Who are you?"

"Son of Chaos."

"No longer," she replied. "Who are you, Xai? Look deep, consider my words. You are an Archangel's son no longer, but an Archangel yourself. And you are destined to lead with Evangeline at your side."

I laid my head against his chest, my ear resting just over his heart. *For eternity.*

I knew you weren't mad at me anymore.

Oh, I am, but you'll make it up to me after this cryptic conversation ends.

His palm moved to my lower back, his wings brushing mine in an almost soothing manner. *You love me.*

I do, I agreed softly. *Even when I want to kill you.*

"Stop flirting with one another and think," his mother chided. "The answer is there. Right at the cusp of your thoughts. Why did Evangeline survive the Shadow realm? She was there for far longer than both of you realize. Why was she able to sprout wings in the underworld?"

Xai studied me for a long moment before saying, "Our deepening bond. She borrowed my darkness and chaos, thus allowing her to thrive in a world she would otherwise suffocate in."

"Yes, now dig deeper," she encouraged, sounding excited. "Who are you, son?"

Ancient energy danced in his midnight irises, causing the hair along my arms to rise. Electricity hummed across his skin, his potential rising to the surface. "You wish for me to remain in Heaven." The words were spoken with finality, as if he already saw the path ahead of him.

"It's the will of the fates, yes."

"Because this is just the beginning," he added, reminding me of Lucía's warning to Alastor. "The ancients are no longer strong enough to uphold the balance. That's the movement I felt earlier, not harm befalling Heaven but power shifting into others—me."

"Yes." Anticipation underlined that solitary word. "Tell me, Xai."

His eyes found mine again, that ancient energy leaving his midnight eyes. "I'm the Archangel of Shadows, and Evangeline is my Consort of Shadows."

Umm...

"And my work here is done," his mother said, sounding relieved. "Enjoy your evening. We'll chat more in the morning, I'm sure."

The sound of her feathers had my jaw dropping more than Xai's words. Had she just laid a bombshell at our door and... left?

Here's your destiny outlined. Have fun! Oh, and you have new titles. Hope you like them. Cheers.

"That's fairly typical of my mother," Xai murmured, sounding not nearly as alarmed as I felt.

"Consort of Shadows?" I repeated. "And did your mother pretty much just tell us the fate of the world is in our hands, and good luck with that?"

He nodded. "That's how I interpreted it, yes." He drew

his hand up and down my back. "And I rather like your new title, Consort."

I snorted. "Okay, Archangel."

"I like the way that sounds."

"Don't get used to it."

"Oh, I think I will." He nuzzled my nose, his grin obnoxiously charming. "I was worried for a moment my mother might proclaim me a Prince of Hell."

"No, just King of the Shadow Realm, apparently."

He frowned, considering. "I suppose that makes sense, and why I can see all of Hell's realms. I always assumed it to be related to my chaotic birthright, but it's tied to destiny too."

"'*You embody the gray. Both entities in one,*'" I said, repeating his mother's cryptic words. "Huh. She sometimes makes sense."

I wrapped my legs around his waist as he lifted me into his arms. "She's always been a puppet master, hence our stay on Earth. She was preparing us for our role here, but there's a benefit to the upgrade."

He carried me through the threshold, his direction confirming we were headed for the bedroom. "Does it involve fucking?" I asked, knowing his one-track mind.

"Absolutely," he murmured, his lips brushing mine. "With wings, Evangeline. Because if we're staying here, we can keep our feathers."

My heart skipped a beat, elation warming my blood. I'd missed flying more than anything in my existence, and I knew Xai felt the same. "But what about the Dark Provenance and our responsibilities on Earth?"

"Something tells me we're expected to do both," he replied, laying me on his bed, his body settling over mine. "But with far more visits up here." He went to his elbows on either side of my head, his gaze serious. "We could say no, love. I can't say what will happen if we do, but it is one of the paths."

"Say no to everything and just run away to be together?" I whispered. "Actually retire, you mean?"

"Yes," he replied just as softly. "We could go wherever you wanted, hide from everyone and everything, and be us. Only us."

"It's tempting," I admitted.

"It is."

"And wrong," I added.

"It is," he repeated.

I sighed, hating all this destiny crap. "Why can't the demons and angels just play nice and be friends?"

"Because that would be boring."

Well, that was true. I drew my hand along his feathers, luxuriating in their silky texture. "I do like you in this form."

"Naked?"

"And with wings." I smiled, fondling the strength of him. "If we stay, could we get a place together outside of the city? One where your mother can't just drop by when I'm naked?" It was a reasonable concern since it had happened twice now.

"A place like our home in the mountains, you mean?"

I nodded. "With an arsenal and a place for sparring."

Amusement flitted through his expression. "Foreplay is one of my favorite pastimes."

"I know." My lips tilted to match his. "I'll need a room for my knives."

"Now you're just trying to seduce me," he murmured.

I feigned innocence. "It's a fair request. I need somewhere to train and perfect my techniques."

He groaned, his lips falling to my neck. "Evangeline," he growled.

"What? You know how much I love practicing my throws."

He bit my pulse, hard, causing me to arch into him, more than ready for his brand of loving.

"Is that a yes?" I whispered. "To us procuring our own place?" His home was nice, but I would prefer to have one that I could call *ours*, something we never needed, thanks to living on Earth all this time.

He took my mouth in a searing kiss, burning me from the inside out. Heavens, he fucked with his tongue the way he did with his body, and I adored it. So dominant. So hot. So *mine*.

"Yes," he said harshly, his lips possessing mine. "Yes to it all, Evangeline."

"For eternity?"

"For eternity."

A vow.

A future.

A love worth the world and more.

"I love you, Archangel of Shadows."

"I love you too, Consort of Shadows."

The Dark Provenance Series concludes with *Captive of Hell*, featuring Trudy and Ashmedai.

Thank you for reading!!

I made a deal with a Prince of Hell.
And now I'm his mate.

All I asked for was my freedom after being captured and
dragged down to the underworld.
Prince Ashmedai agreed to the terms in exchange for a
blood vow.
A blood vow that I belatedly realized tied our souls together
for eternity.

Oh, I'm free all right.
Free to roam his realm.
To live in Hell for the rest of my very long life.
Or short life, according to the infamous *Grim Reaper*.

Because, yeah, it's never a good sign when the demon in
charge of the afterlife says he'll be seeing you soon.
If only I had someone in my life who could help.

Like my absentee Archangel father or my devious
Archdemon mate.
Alas, no. That's not how fate works in my world.

The veil is about to fall.
The realms are on the verge of collective chaos.
And the power inside me is the key to our salvation.

I just might have to die in the process to release it.
Something Prince Ashmedai has known all along.
For he's the one wielding the blade.
Essentially holding my life in his proverbial hands.

How about another deal, Archdemon?
Save me and I'll help you save the world.
Kill me and I'll take you down with me.
What'll it be?

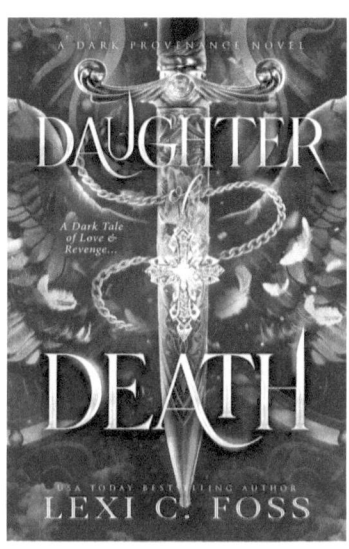

An award-winning paranormal romance featuring a retired assassin, her former lover, and their penchant for playing with knives.

A dead body.
A missing daughter.
A silver blade.

All the clues point to one person: Me.

My name is Evangeline, and I'm a fallen angel who wants nothing to do with the underworld. But an edict from a Demonic Lord forces me to return to the man and the life I left behind.

I have seven days to prove my innocence.
Whoever set me up is going to die.

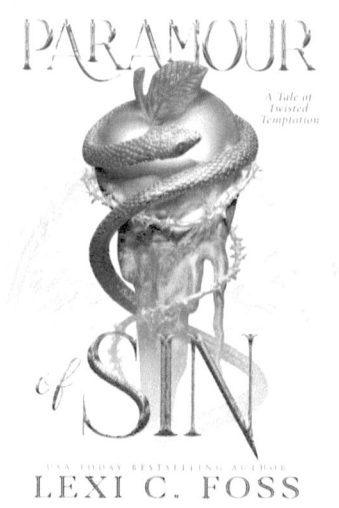

PARAMOUR

A Tale of
Twisted
Temptation

of SIN

USA TODAY BESTSELLING AUTHOR

LEXI C. FOSS

Gwen is a succubus with a control problem. What happens when a Demonic Lord and a sexy incubus try to help her out? A threesome, of course.

A dead conquest.
A Succubus signature.
An edict sending the culprit back to Hell.

The culprit being me.

My name is Gwen, and I'm a Succubus with a control problem. Except I didn't create this mess.

Now I have twelve days to prove my innocence.
Not a problem.
Well, minus one minor detail—the two hot demons hell-bent on helping me prove my case.

Lord Zebulon makes me want to fall to my knees with a single glance.
And Zane recently shattered my heart.

It's a match made in Hell. And a union probably blessed by the devil himself.

So I have twelve days not to fall in love.
Twelve days of staying out of Zane's and Lord Zebulon's beds.
And twelve days to find out who framed me for murder.

Man, sometimes being a Succubus really sucks.

Author's Note: *Paramour of Sin* is a standalone paranormal romance featuring a Demonic Lord with a penchant for drawing blood, a kinky Incubus with a proclivity for playing dirty, and a wayward Succubus known for her lethal touch. There will be MM, MF, and MMF content.

A standalone enemies-to-lovers paranormal romance.

A lifetime of vengeance and decades of pain...

He abandoned her in Hell. She's returned to make him pay.

Kay

Once upon a time, I fell for an Archangel's trick.
He bonded me to him for eternity.
Then left me in Hell to survive alone.

I'm no longer the woman I was before.
I'm stronger. Faster. Harder. And lethal.

It's my turn to deliver justice where it's due.
I'm coming for you, Archangel Ezra.
And your precious Divinity, too.

Ezra

Once upon a time, I seduced a demon Halfling into helping me save the balance.

I engaged in a sacred bond.

Then I abandoned her without a word.

I'm no longer the Archangel I was before.

I'm broken. Suffering. Destroyed by my *mate*.

Now she's coming for me, wielding a blade with the intent to kill.

I won't kneel for you, Princess of Bael.

And I'm prepared to fight.

Author's Note: *Princess of Bael* is a standalone paranormal romance in the Dark Provenance world, which can be read in any order. This novel contains violent elements and sensual material. Kay's deadly. Ezra's deadlier. A match made in literal hell. Forbidden. Fun. And darkly delicious.

Acknowledgments

First and foremost, to my husband for tolerating my very late hours and all the conversations I hold in my head. I love you <3

Allison: Seriously, I would be lost with you. Thank you for always being there for me, listening to my ideas, paying attention to all the little details, pointing out my repetition, and for reading *Son of Chaos* in such a brief period of time!

Bethany: Thank you for editing this book in pieces for me! I'm sorry for the minor heart attacks, cliffhangers, and inspiring your need to write fan fiction at times (to resurrect certain characters). I love working with you!

Barb & Delphine: Thank you both for always reviewing my work with a critical eye, proofing all my words, and offering invaluable feedback. You've both become a vital part of my team and I appreciate you ladies more than I can say.

Louise & Melissa: You both keep my social media pages alive, but more importantly, you keep me thriving. Your friendships mean the world to me - Thank you!

Amy, Barb, Joy, Laura, Louise, Sarah & Tracey: Thank you all for reading *Son of Chaos* and providing invaluable feedback.

Y'all don't let me off the hook easily and I LOVE that. Thank you!

Famous Owls: Thank you all for your continued support, comments, and positive energy. You all make me smile daily :)

None of this could be possible without my ARC team and Foss's Night Owls. Thank you, thank you, thank you!

And to the readers: Thank you for reading *Son of Chaos*. I hope you enjoyed hearing from Evangeline and Xai again as I suspect they have at least another book coming in this series...

USA Today Bestselling Author Lexi C. Foss loves to play in dark worlds, especially the ones that bite. She lives in North Carolina with her family. When not writing, she's busy crossing items off her travel bucket list, or chasing eclipses around the globe. She's quirky, consumes way too much coffee, and loves to swim.

Where To Find Lexi:
www.LexiCFoss.com

ALSO BY LEXI C. FOSS

Blood Alliance Series - Dystopian Paranormal

Chastely Bitten

Royally Bitten

Regally Bitten

Rebel Bitten

Kingly Bitten

Cruelly Bitten

Blood Alliance Standalones - Dystopian Paranormal

Blood Day

Crave Me

Dark Provenance Series - Paranormal Romance

Heiress of Bael (FREE!)

Daughter of Death

Paramour of Sin

Princess of Bael

Son of Chaos

Captive of Hell

Elemental Fae Academy - Reverse Harem

Book One

Book Two

Book Three

Elemental Fae Queen

Winter Fae Queen

Hell Fae - Reverse Harem

Hell Fae Captive

Hell Fae Warden

Immortal Curse Series - Paranormal Romance

Book One: Blood Laws

Book Two: Forbidden Bonds

Book Three: Blood Heart

Book Four: Blood Bonds

Book Five: Angel Bonds

Book Six: Blood Seeker

Book Seven: Wicked Bonds

Book Eight: Blood King

Immortal Curse World - Short Stories & Bonus Fun

Elder Bonds

Blood Burden

Assassin Bonds

Mershano Empire Series - Contemporary Romance

Book One: The Prince's Game

Book Two: The Charmer's Gambit

Book Three: The Rebel's Redemption

Midnight Fae Academy - Reverse Harem

Ella's Masquerade

Book One

Book Two

Book Three

Book Four

Noir Reformatory - Ménage Paranormal Romance

The Beginning

First Offense

Second Offense

Third Offense

Fourth Offense

Underworld Royals Series - Dark Paranormal Romance

Happily Ever Crowned

Happily Ever Bitten

X-Clan Series - Dystopian Paranormal

Andorra Sector

X-Clan: The Experiment

Winter's Arrow

Bariloche Sector

V-Clan Series - Dystopian Paranormal

Blood Sector

Night Sector

Vampire Dynasty - Dark Paranormal

Violet Slays

Crossed Fates

Other Books

Scarlet Mark - Standalone Romantic Suspense

Rotanev - Standalone Poseidon Tale

Carnage Island - Standalone Reverse Harem Romance

www.ingramcontent.com/pod-product-compliance
Lightning Source LLC
Chambersburg PA
CBHW022008170626
46808CB00001B/324